Live Life

SHAME ON YOU!

SHAME ON YOU!

Story By

LARRY GONZALES

Written By

Mark Villasenor
Larry Shannon
and
Larry Gonzales

authorHOUSE®

AuthorHouse™
1663 Liberty Drive
Bloomington, IN 47403
www.authorhouse.com
Phone: 1 (800) 839-8640

Published by AuthorHouse   05/24/2016

ISBN: 978-1-5049-4943-9 (sc)
ISBN: 978-1-5049-4944-6 (hc)
ISBN: 978-1-5049-4942-2 (e)

Library of Congress Control Number: 2015914852

Print information available on the last page.

Any people depicted in stock imagery provided by Thinkstock are models, and such images are being used for illustrative purposes only. Certain stock imagery © Thinkstock.

This book is printed on acid-free paper.

Because of the dynamic nature of the Internet, any web addresses or links contained in this book may have changed since publication and may no longer be valid. The views expressed in this work are solely those of the author and do not necessarily reflect the views of the publisher, and the publisher hereby disclaims any responsibility for them.

Acknowledgements

Edited by
Kirstan Villasenor
and
Gabby Ciarmella

1
REFLECTION

"Dad, you there?"

"Yeah Sweetie, where are you? You ok?"

"No, dad, I'm a little freaked. We're in the limo and I just told Brooklyn and Aubrey that I don't think I can go through with it. They told me to call you."

"Lindsay, you don't have to do anything you don't want to do. We can just have the reception. No pressure."

"Dad, listen to me... Gotcha dad!

"OOOHHHHHH!! That's funny. Ok, put Brooklyn on. So whose idea was that, hers or yours?"

"We both came up with that simultaneously. You should see Aubrey. She is still laughing her round head off."

"You got me good. Listen, I put the airline and honeymoon info on..."

"Got it"

"Luke was supposed to..."

"He did, everything is taken care of. You can relax now."

"Ok see you in a little bit."

I really don't remember much about that day until after I got that call. I mean, I'm used to Brooklyn taking care of most everything. Once I hung up the cell phone, I apologized to the other customers in the restaurant for the exploding laugh and ordered dessert. It wasn't that I was nervous. I was ecstatic that Lindsay and Lee were getting married after all this time. I was sweating a little bit, even though it was an overcast, late fall afternoon. But I was sweating mostly because of this tux that felt four sizes too big. Every detail is ingrained in my mind. The excitement of waiting for the family to get to the chapel, the anticipation of seeing Kaylee and Jack and them being a part of this big day after so many years of the relationships we never had; it was all coming to a head. So I finished my plate, paid the tab and walked down the street to the chapel, ready to give my daughter away.

One by one, the guests on the small list arrived. Short but sweet was the list, which could also be used to describe the chapel. Lindsay was so adamant about wanting very little help with the planning of the wedding and all the details that went along with it. She has always been amazing. Brooklyn has been amazing. But putting this all together in just three months, all the touches of color, flowers and little details, they are truly talented. The ceremony was exactly what Lindsay wanted: delicate, full of color and a party of family and close friends. She didn't want any more or any less.

Nobody deserves to be happier than Lindsay. Nobody has come as far as Lindsay has come, with everything that has gone on in the past dozen or so years. Of course, Aubrey and Luke also went through the tough times, but Lindsay was old enough to remember a lot of what went on. Most would say that she was forced to grow up faster than any kid should have to grow up. But even to this day, I still see the girl who I used to sing to sleep after changing her extremely dirty diapers.

My thoughts as the music began and the procession started were how lucky I am to be here with the people I love and need more than anything in the world. I peek around the corner to see Luke walk Brooklyn down the aisle. In twelve years, Brooklyn has become the rock of our household and best mother these kids could have. I see that she now fits in with the rest of the extended family. Tight knit families can be tough to become a part of, especially when there is no formal event like a wedding to solidify it for everyone to see. Especially when my family has seen the kids and I go through devastation and anguish. The times I see the kids introduce Brooklyn as their mom, I don't know who is prouder, her or me.

I see Luke as the young man he has become and Brooklyn is the reason he is such a caring person. I wish that Luke had a sibling or even a cousin that was closer to his age to push and challenge him in a different way than we do. I know that he will find his way with his schooling and go on to accomplish big things.

When it comes to Aubrey, I see both sides of the spectrum. I see the good in her. I see how beautiful she is inside and out. I see that she is putting her life together as an adult and is off to such a good start. But I often wonder how much she remembers. I wonder if she has more of her mother in her than me. I am very confident in the ways Brooklyn and I raised her, but is it enough to instill long term stability in a young woman who has often times been a follower rather than a leader? I love her, just like all my kids, and I probably haven't said it enough to Kaylee and Jack. But for some reason, I worry about Aubrey a little more than her siblings. Today though, she is walking down the aisle as Lindsay's maid of honor.

"You ready dad? Dad?"

"Yeah sweetie, let's do it."

And the music began. I couldn't ever be prouder. My baby girl was walking down the aisle to the man of her dreams. A very good man who I know will provide a good life for her. That's all a dad can really ask for. I just wanted to make sure she never wanted for anything. I wanted to protect her from the bad things in the world. I wanted to show her that "family first" should always take precedence. And I wanted her to find a man who would continue to do that for her as a loving, supportive equal and best friend. I know she will be happy with Lee. As I literally gave her away, I kissed her on the cheek and she gave me that smile that I have been accustomed to get from Lindsay.

The ceremony was also short and sweet. I couldn't quite make out what music was playing in the background from the wedding in the next room. What can you expect from a tiny chapel near the corner of Wilshire and La Brea? In just a few short minutes and vows, my Lindsay gave up her last name for a new one. Dozens of pictures later, we were on our way to the reception hall for some food, not to mention an open bar, waiting for us.

Seeing Lindsay and Lee dance their first dance as husband and wife, it was the perfect ending to an amazing day for everyone. Everyone but me. You see, I had to have my last dance with Lindsay Martinez. It's my right and privilege as father of the bride to have those few minutes with her. As I heard the lyrics to the song, "I loved her first," I felt that this was my perfect ending. I could now officially give her away. After all, I did love her first. Before anyone knew about her, before she came into the world. As soon as I found out that a baby was coming in July, I loved her at that very moment.

So I hugged her a few seconds and kissed her one last time as the music was ending. As she walked away, albeit just to the sweethearts' table, a tear began to build in my eye. It went away very quickly as Lindsay turned back and gave me that smile that only Lindsay could. Then it hit me like an eight-foot wave at Zuma beach. That smile, I have seen it before, and it took me back right then and there.

It also happened to come in July, just like Lindsay, but unlike her wedding day, that day was extremely hot and the tux was too tight. I was extremely nervous, just as any twenty-one year old kid can get when he is about to take one woman as his wife for the rest of his life. I was almost to the point of vomiting. Unlike what most would expect it had nothing to do with many, many drinks the night before.

You see, I woke up that day in a very cold sweat, mostly because my friends left me to pass out on the floor in nothing but my tighty-whiteys right next to the air conditioner. It was a miracle that I could even get up after one last hurrah with my buddies on the town as a single man. Naturally each one of them took their turn to embarrass me and tell anyone in the bar who would listen about my escapades as a "Casanova." What can I say? I had fun, lots of fun. And what I didn't know back then was that, while girls are a lot of fun, girls can get you killed.

However, I was ready to put that all behind me and walk down the aisle. Yet way, way back in my mind, I knew that it was a mistake. Was she "the one?" Did I turn my back on the actual "one?" Is it my obligation to meet her at the front of the church? Will I be letting my parents down if I don't do the right thing? I mean, hell, I tried on the wedding band a couple weeks before and it felt as heavy as an eight-pound shot put. Perhaps that shot put found its way to the pit of my stomach. As I was getting ready, which wouldn't take so long except my hair needs extra attention and just the right amount of coiffing, all of this was weighing on my mind as well as my stomach. I couldn't shake the feeling though. I sat there looking in the mirror trying to convince myself that many other grooms have those same cold-feet thoughts.

I decided to take a drive. As I came to a stop light on my way to the church I saw that the digital thermometer on the bank building showed an eye popping 107. Part of me wanted to take a detour to the beach and catch some waves. My surfboard was in the truck bed wrapped in a blanket I got at a party. Had brand new surfboard wax from Tuesday. Even the Beach Boys "Don't Worry Baby" was cranked up on the radio and I had my work tools holding my board in place. But there was something I had to do. The music started to fade out in favor of my thoughts as I got out of the car and knocked on the door. It only took a few seconds before the door opened, but it had been a few weeks since I began having these second thoughts. I needed to come clean, pour my heart out one last time and say a final goodbye to my past. It made me feel a little better. It didn't completely ease my worries, but nonetheless I took off for the church to face my future.

Unlike Lindsay's wedding, I got to the church and knew that hundreds of our closest friends were waiting for me. In the foyer, I caught a glimpse of a sign that read, "Rick Martinez to marry Rachel Parker today." It just didn't look right. As I made my way to the back, I passed by numerous happy, familiar faces wishing me luck, shaking my hand, and kissing my cheek. I couldn't tell you who any of them were at this point. All I wanted to do was get to the waiting room and have a cold one before I took my place between the altar and the congregation. I faced the altar first and took a couple of deep breaths. I could feel all of the eyes on the back of my neck and the hair on it stood straight up. The song began, "Here Comes the Bride," and I turned around. While I could see Rachel's smile through her veil, my life was literally flashing before my eyes. My name is Rick Martinez and this is my story.

2
FOUNDATION

Anybody who tells you that working construction is fun, don't believe them. Nobody ever says "I want to be a construction worker when I grow up." That's not how I saw my life. But nonetheless, that's the life I had after high school. And five months past my twenty-first birthday, I was still doing it, making pretty good money from it too. So at least there was some benefit. The job certainly does not make you excited to get up in the morning. Especially when you have to get to the job site before the rooster crows and even then, there is always someone there ahead of you waiting impatiently for you to arrive. I remember those days like they were yesterday.

There was on time. There was earlier than on time. And then there was Dad time, which I was taught growing up. However, I had grown accustomed to Dad time at work. Well, let me rephrase, I had suffered through Dad time. This man, Armand, as the world knows him, had owned the family construction company for twenty-something years. A Silver Star recipient from the Korean War, Dad could do it all. He could fish, he could hunt, he was a damn good mechanic, he always provided for the family, and years later, he still works harder than any three men I know. There are days I can't stand him. But growing up, I saw the foundation he was laying for me, my older brother and my older sister. I love him more than words can say. When it comes to the Martinez family, he is the unquestioned leader. And whenever I pull up to any job site, past or present, it takes me back to the normal exchanges with my dad.

"Get your ass in here, you're late!" I couldn't ask for a better alarm clock, "Don't we open this job site at six, damn it?!"

As I get out of my truck and scan the job site, in the dark mind you, and see absolutely no one and nothing. Well nothing but those piercing eyes of his. I can only muster up a shot of sarcasm.

"Yes we do and it's a good thing."

"Where were you last night?"

"Out."

In my mind, I know the script by now.

"You get any sleep?"

"A little. Met up with some buddies and crashed on their couch."

"So that means you met a piece of ass and you crashed on their couch afterward?"

"Normally yes, but I knew I had to be here at six this morning"

"You smoking pot?"

"No, Dad."

"Why should I believe you?"

"Because you scare the hell out of me! I worry about any beating from you more than any sentence a cop or judge could slap on me."

He stands for a moment then retorts:

"Ok start by measuring those two-by-fours…"

Deep down, I was laughing and biting my lip. Yet measuring those beams, I would think about the what-ifs. Just a few years prior I was playing soccer in Europe. Actually, I was dominating. Our team was dominating. We were beating all the European teams and I was on cloud nine. That was until I got caught drinking and was benched by my coach, my dad. I was a great soccer player. This was back when soccer was just becoming popular in the States and just entering the high schools as a legitimate sports program. When playing for the local leagues or against other schools in the area, it felt like the parting of the Red Sea. I could hear the whispers. I could hear the people talking, "There he goes. There goes Rick Martinez, the best player in the area." Not only was it a great feeling, it was a great time.

My brother, who was studying to be an accountant at one of the top universities in the country, had arranged for me to meet with their soccer coach. Right away I was offered a scholarship to play division one college soccer. I mentioned that my grades were sub-par. His words, "We'll take care of it." I thought about it, but at the end of the day, school just wasn't for me. I just wanted to party. Party and play soccer on my terms, no responsibilities. I just wanted to run up and down the field and find a different way each game to knock the ball into the back of the net. When I missed, I could hear another voice. A very high pitched voiced, "Oh Rick, how could you miss that one?!" I'd look to the sidelines and see my mom with her hand on her forehead, then leaning back in disbelief. Sometimes she would lean back so far, her wig would come off and everybody would break into laughter. Even Dad would joke, "You better pick up some chili dogs, she's not making dinner for us tonight."

Those dinners. Those lunches. Hell, every meal Mom made was just the best homemade Mexican food you could ever taste. Chorizo and eggs for breakfast. Leftovers for lunch, which typically meant taco meat, cheese, beans and corn tortillas. For dinner, you name it. Chili con carne one night, enchiladas the next. Food that was all made with recipes handed down from generation to generation. Helen, as her friends knew her, was the best cook in the land. She would always make sure I had clothes to wear, food to eat and a few dollars to have fun with. I teased her constantly about her high pitched voice, especially when she'd get excited or mad. I'd leave early on a summer morning to go surfing and could hear the yell from half a block away,

"Be careful mijo and be home by three." Naturally, I'd pull in the driveway at four.

"Rick, get your ass in here! You're never going surfing again!" She'd yell.

"Just calm down, I'm ok, nothing bad happened. I wasn't doing anything I'm not supposed to do. I am just late."

"You better clean up and hope your father doesn't find out you were an hour late. By the way mijo, did you pick up the sothas like I asked?"

"Yes Mom, I got the so-das."

"You know what I mean. Keep making fun of me, you're gonna miss me when I'm gone!"

That's Mom to a tee. Her Spanish accent is so cute and so easy to make fun of. Sodas are an everyday occurrence. A spatula is spashla. But no one can deny that she was a good wife. He was a good husband and treated her wonderfully. But those day-to-day spats and normal married-life conflicts, sometimes I say deserves a medal. She was the best mother too, raised the three of us and provided us with a happy home.

In my eyes, my dad was always on my case. My older brother and older sister would say something like, "Are you kidding Rick?! You got it easy." Mom would then add, "That's right mijo, I don't care how old you are, you'll always be my baby." And there you had it. How can you argue with that? How can you argue with any of it? They taught me how to fish, taught me how to water ski, taught me how to fight, taught me how to cook, and taught me how to pour concrete. More than anything, they taught me how to be a man. I don't know what I'd do without them. And just when I'm letting all these warm and fuzzy thoughts swim around in my head, I'd hear banging all around the job site and snap back to reality, thanks to Dad…

"Damn it Rick, what are you doing? You're supposed to saw off a half inch, not an eighth of an inch. Go get the other two-by-fours and the skilsaw in the truck and do it again. And this time, pay attention to what you are doing."

Around lunch time on the jobsite, it would never fail. My brother would show up. The college graduate, wrapped in his sporty Fiat, dropping in to say hi to Dad and I. Here I was in nothing but some ripped jeans and a tank top while he exits the car in some nice designer slacks, leather jacket (even if it was a warm day), and a polo shirt. Dad would bee line over to him, give him a big hug and ask him about college life or life in corporate America.

How can I best describe my brother Gil? In my mind, he was the golden child. I guess a combination of Steve McQueen and Mr. Wizard would sum it up. Or, a real life Evel Knievel meets Donald Trump. He's four years older than me. We used to have so many good times riding bikes through the neighborhood or taking turns water skiing at Lake Powell. But there were also days we would be on completely different wave lengths. The days I would be at the soccer field, he was at home watching a Twilight Zone marathon. I'd be at my friend's house partying; he'd be studying all night for a big test. You see, the truth is, the main difference between him and I was discipline. I have it today but not back then. In fact, had it been common in the 1970's, I would probably have been diagnosed with Attention Deficit Disorder. My brother was a great student; straight A's most of his school years but also a pretty decent athlete. He played soccer and handball, but his best sport was swimming. I never understood how he would get up in the morning and before taking a swim, he would take a shower.

Make no mistake; Gil also had some luck with the ladies. Especially when he went off to college, which was only an hour away, where he joined a fraternity. He had his fair share of ladies sneaking out of his room in the middle of the night to make that infamous walk back to their sorority or other on campus living space. But overall, Gil would rather play on the Atari instead of going to the beach. He would rather drive fast cars than work on them. He'd prefer a Tom Collins over a beer. When working, he's very intense and desires to make a lot of money. Deep down though, he is a gentleman and a family man. He and I used to get a kick out of seeing how much trouble we could get out of and how much we would tease our sister.

To know Beth is to love her. But to know her is to push just the right buttons for just the right amount of time to get her heated. If there was ever a middle child syndrome or middle child scenario, Beth is living proof. The only daughter of our mom and dad, she took the brunt of us boys but also took the brunt of having an extremely over-protective father.

Like the rest of us, my sister was also a pretty good athlete. She water skied and played softball and soccer. In fact, she had one of the longest throw-ins I have ever seen from a women's soccer player. Not bad for a little girl at 5'4" and barely 100 pounds. But I guess the main thing I had in common with her was that school was just not for us. That and the fact we've been known to fight on the soccer field. We wouldn't start the fights, but we certainly would end them.

Boy my sister was tough. You did not want to cross her at all. Definitely something she got from my boss. Most of the time we didn't get along. I can remember one time she was mad at me about something, probably because I was tugging on her pony tail. She chased me down and cornered me up against my bedroom door and tried to punch me. Well, lucky for me, I moved and she missed. Unlucky for her, I moved and she hit the doorknob and broke her finger. How did we know it was broken? The bone from her pinky finger was pushing against the skin. Although it did take Mom a full day to admit that Beth had a broken bone, she finally took her to the emergency room. It was a typical brother-sister relationship. We didn't like each other, but we loved each other when necessary.

That love was seen when we were on a camping trip in Utah. We had just finished a full day of skiing and were unloading the boat to take all the stuff back to camp. Beth grabbed Dad's brand new ski and a couple of chairs. I can still hear Dad's voice, "You better not drop that ski, it costs more than your sixteen years!" As she starting walking, she passed a couple of bushes and the ski clipped the bush. That bush happened to contain a swarm of mosquitoes that attacked her. When I say swarm, I don't mean a few. I'm talking about hundreds. In a matter of seconds, she had ballooned up like a giant tomato. We dropped everything and took her to the local hospital. I can still remember overhearing the doctor tell Mom and Dad that if we waited another few minutes her airway would have closed. I saw my parents embrace around the same time that my brother and I embraced. We were lucky. Beth was lucky, and at that moment, I knew just how much I loved my sister and my family. You wish it didn't have to come to something like that but when you're a teenager, you just don't realize that tomorrow isn't guaranteed. I knew from then on, and was reminded over and over in my life, that you have to tell the loved ones in your life just how much you care for them.

That was just one of many trips we would take as a family. Sometimes we would go with friends. Sometimes we would go with extended family. But for the most part, it was the five of us. Sure, Dad and I used to take off on our own and go fishing in Canada and all over the western United States. But when I look back on my childhood, especially my teen years, our weekends were always busy. We could be on a surf trip up the coast of Ventura. We could be in our camper listening to Hank Williams or Roger Miller. We could be at the soccer field. Some of the best times were when Mom and Dad went to Vegas to see Frank Sinatra and the Rat Pack, leaving us kids at home. So we partied. And we had a wonderful party house.

It was a normal house until you got to the family room. Dad had his deer and antelope heads along with his rifles mounted over the fireplace and a big TV, well big for the 1970's. Past the family room was the game room, which had the nicest pool table around. You've heard of Minnesota Fats? Well you see, I was California Skinny and earned more than a few bucks whenever someone thought they were better than me. Past the game room was the door to the back yard. The back yard didn't have a huge lawn, although we did have enough room for a big orange tree and lemon tree. But the main attraction was the almost Olympic size pool equipped with slide and diving board. This is where the party was when our parents were out of town, but even when they were in town, we often decided to stay home on the weekends.

Dad worked hard. Mom worked hard helping him keep the company books and keep the house clean. But they knew how to have fun on the weekends. Gil, Beth and I had our chores just like other kids. We split the chores for the most part. Keeping our own rooms clean, that went without saying. We also had to keep the bathrooms clean, help with the kitchen, the front lawn, and especially with the pool. But the one chore we loved to do was to pick up after Rags.

When you hear about a cute, lovable beagle, everyone thinks of Snoopy. The Martinez family had Rags. Dad had a stretch when he would bring home a stray dog once in a while, to which Mom would reply, "No, take it away" as if it were trash. For some reason, when Dad brought Rags home, Mom replied, "Just for tonight." I was five when Rags became part of the family and she was definitely part of the family. She was with us on all of our camping trips. She slept in our beds. Sometimes she would go to work with Dad. She was a great dog. Rags wasn't dirty, she didn't shed much. She had just the cutest personality. In fact to this day, I have a framed picture of her lying by the pool on a beach towel, donning a hat and sunglasses.

However, that pool became difficult for her. From inside the house we could hear her whimper as she got older and fell in the pool repeatedly. There were times we weren't home and she would fall in. Luckily for us, our neighbors would climb over the wall and rescue her. She had bad hips and started to go blind. So one day, after many trips to the vet, Dad told Beth and me to take Rags and put her down. She was just too old and was suffering too much. We started to cry. Gil was away at college. Beth was eighteen. I was fifteen and was lucky enough to have not gone through any losses that close to home up until then. We certainly weren't going to be a part of it. So Dad decided to do it, but at the last minute I could see the tears well up in his eyes. That was the first time I ever saw that tough man shed tears. So he asked a family friend to do it. Mom came home later from a day of shopping. Ironically, once she got in the house and put the groceries on the kitchen counter she said,

"Rags, I have a treat for you. Come here Rags."

Dad with his head down said, "Rags isn't here anymore."

Right away she broke down and cried, "NO! How could you do that?!"

She knew deep down that was the right thing to do. That weekend, my brother Gil came home from college. We hadn't told him anything yet. He walked in the door, gave us all a hug and called out for Rags. All of us started crying. He knew right then and there that Rags was gone and began crying too. Rags was fifteen. So was I.

The day when Rags was put down was one of the few times I saw the soft side of my dad. After that, I became accustomed to the dad that was my boss, the one telling me to re-cut the 2-by-4's that day I messed up while lost in thought.

At the end of that long day of construction I found myself counting the minutes till I could go home. I couldn't sprint to my truck, was too tired and sore to do that. So as I slowly made my way to the truck, Dad asked me to stop at the mini-mart and pick up some cigarettes for him. He also asked me to tell Mom to start dinner and that he would be home by six. On the way home, there was a part of me that wanted to go out. It was a Friday night and I just got paid. But I already had a motorcycle trip planned in the morning, so I decided I was just going to go home and crash. I got to the mini mart and as I was walking through the parking lot I spotted that white convertible MG. Seeing the faded Fleetwood Mac bumper sticker, it confirmed what I already knew. I looked up, saw her walk out the door and walk straight towards me. So much for the cigarettes.

3
BACHELORHOOD

I'll never be able to tell you what Shelley was wearing that day in the parking lot but I guarantee this, I'll never forget how she looked. She looked as wonderful as the day we met. Ironically enough, her reaction to me now was pretty similar to the reaction she had when we first met. She didn't look that happy to see me. You see, Shelley was not only beautiful, but very intelligent and very aware of each situation. She knew I was "that guy." You know the type; single, always wanting to party, always wanting the variety, always wanting the fun. Never wanting to deal with anything or anyone who wasn't about that.

And before I could say anything that day, she came up with the perfect Shelley greeting.

"Your ears must have been ringing today, my sister and I had lunch earlier and we were going over the times you were such an asshole." She said with a deviant smile.

"And here I thought my ears were ringing from all the women who were reminiscing about how much fun I was. Either that or the skilsaw at the job today."

"You still working for your dad?"

"Yep. It's a never ending hell."

"Aww, and how are Mom and Dad? I miss them."

"They're doing well, nothing ever changes. You should drop by the house and say hi sometime. I know my mom would love to see you."

"Probably not a good idea."

"Why not?"

"Rick, you know why not."

I did know, but the devil in me wanted to hear the words. Shelley was an equal to me. If I had put on an album, not only did she know what it was before it started playing, but she would request the song I was planning to put on. If we were going to grab a bite to eat, she'd pick the restaurant I wanted. But more than anything she challenged me. She was way different than the other girls I had dated.

I was 19 years old when I first caught a glimpse of her while she was working at a store in the local mall. It was such a tease because I was working at a men's clothing store just three doors down. Shelley stood 5'4" and had this amazing straight, light brown hair, below shoulder length, piercing brown eyes and great legs. To say the least, she was very well put together.

I thought she was a real bitch. She wasn't really, but at first, she just wouldn't give me the time of day. That was different for me. That made her a challenge. I was going to make her like me no matter what. One thing we did have in common was the fact that we both loved to be dressed to the nines. When I finally got the courage to talk to her, she was very short with me. A lot of one word answers. I couldn't tell if that was just how she was or if she was purposely making me work hard for every word. It really got on my nerves. After a few times, she began to lighten up. Was I making some progress or was it just useless to keep up these shenanigans? I decided to take a shot and invite her to a party I was going to on the weekend. To my surprise she said, "I would love to…"

In my mind, I was already celebrating and imagining what I was going to wear.

"But I already have plans. Sorry."

Ouch! What a blow to my ego. Did I wait too long or was she just being polite? It didn't happen too much in the past, but of course I had been turned down before, and in the past it was no big deal. I'd just move on to the next girl. Play the law of averages. But this time, I was a little bothered.

The weekend came and I did go to that party. I took my turn around the room, talking with a few cute girls, doing my normal thing. Seeing who was interested and who I could have the most fun with. An hour went by when I saw a buddy of mine. I went over to give him a hug and as soon as I did, he began his introduction, "Rick I want you to meet my date."

And at the same time I blurted out, "Shelley!" she blurted out, "Rick!" It took me only a few minutes to get her alone. Then after a couple drinks we hit the bedroom for what Sinatra would call, "some ring-a-ding-ding."

Was it great? It was better than that. But it was also different. Shelley introduced me to pillow talk. When I had sex with a girl before, the only thing in my mind was how long I should give her before I should ask her to leave. Or how long should I hold her before I get going. Usually it would be around the five minute mark. Shelley and I were actually having a great conversation which had to have lasted over an hour. And while I'm sure there was loud music in the main room where the party was still going on, it all faded and it seemed to be just Shelley and me. It was at that point when she let her guard down. She proceeded to tell me that from the very beginning I was the guy for her. That it was just a matter of time for her.

Then I realized that Shelley was here with my buddy. I hoped he wouldn't be too pissed. So we got dressed and before we could look for him, he found us and gave us a huge smile.

"Believe it or not, Rick, I was planning on introducing her to you when I made the date. Glad I could help. Here's a beer. Just remember to return the favor someday." That's a damn nice favor.

From that day on, Shelley and I were an item, which to some extent was new to me. Don't get me wrong, I always knew how to treat a lady. It was second nature for me to open doors for girls, compliment them on their hair or their outfit and, of course, pick up the tab on every meal and anything else that had to be paid for. Introducing her to all of my family was also a little new. I brought her by the house one Saturday night after we went out to dinner. Mom, Dad, Gil and Beth were all there, very warm and welcoming to my surprise, especially from Beth. You never know how an older sister is going to view her younger brother's girlfriend. Did I say girlfriend? Yeah, I guess I did.

We all hung out in the family room. I made pina coladas for everyone. We actually got Mom drunk because we were testing all of them out trying to come up with the perfect concoction. You should have heard her high-pitched voice that night after pina colada number three. Dad was even ready to cut her off, which he never did. The family hit it off with her just as easy as her and I hit it off.

While I loved the way she would enjoy dressing up for her man, I also loved that she was very comfortable in a pair of jeans and a sweater. Bottom line, I was falling in love with Shelley. It never really hit me, just a gradual feeling that was so very natural. I could tell she was feeling the same way I was. She became so comfortable with me that she even shared a story that she had never shared with anyone else. Shelley's family had a condo in Mammoth and one time she was slipped a date rape drug by a family friend. Here was this beautiful woman telling me about the most awful moment of her life and I was able to very naturally brush it off and not look at her differently. That told me all I needed to know. A few months went by and I saved up enough dollars to give her a promise ring. I wanted to marry her.

Meeting her family on the other hand, was not so easy. Her mom was very nice but her dad was tough. He was the typical overbearing father. A strong business man who owned a string of nurseries. He was very hard-nosed and would impose his shadow on his daughter and me.

Sometime after that first meeting with her family, I could see the changes. She became very demanding; no doubt her father's influence. Between the two of them, I just felt suffocated. Well, as suffocated as a kid barely out of his teens could possibly feel. I was being pulled in so many different directions, trying to please her and trying to show her dad that I could be the guy for his little girl. Then, for no specific reason, I called her on a Sunday morning.

"I'm calling it off and I'm coming to get my stuff."

I know it sounded very abrupt, which it was. I just panicked, and to some extent, ran away. Well, after I went to her house to get the rest of my stuff, that is.

I knew I hurt her. She couldn't even come out of her room. So I tried something drastic: I went to see her father at work. I simply told him that I felt we were too young. And that tough, macho man consoled me and told me he understood. That made me break down and cry. I had finally won the guy over as I was breaking both his little girl's, and my, heart. Talk about irony.

Shelley and I would talk on the phone for a few weeks, sharing laughs and tears. While I know it was a tough break up for her, in the end she knew I was right. We were too young. And let's not kid ourselves. I wasn't ready to give up the life of a bachelor. Not yet at least.

I don't know how to explain it but from the very first days of high school, girls always seemed to be around. Homecoming night my freshman year, I went home with the homecoming queen… and her friend. From that moment, I had the confidence that women liked in a guy. I didn't impress them with 24 inch biceps. Hell, I was only 5'7" and weighed a puny 135 pounds. I certainly didn't impress them with my mind. And although I was a good athlete, soccer wasn't a sport that women loved all that much. I think the main reason I could always attract girls was that I wanted to have fun and I could make them laugh. Let's face it; if you're a confident guy and you can make a girl laugh, you have a chance with almost any girl.

During high school, Monday morning through Friday afternoon was all about soccer. I guess I made some time for my studies. It was common for me to meet up with whatever girl I was "talking to" at the time during recess and have a little foreplay, just enough to tease her to come back at lunch. And she did. We met at my 1973 Datsun pickup truck in the parking lot and went at it. Sometimes when I knew Mom was out shopping, I would take a girl home at lunch and have my way with her on the living room floor. I might even invite her back after school for a quick round two. And it was only a quick one. After all, I had to go to soccer practice. After school, when there was no soccer, I went surfing or motorcycle riding. Anything to pass the time between women and soccer matches.

Friday night was very much the same each week. It was the only night of the week that Mom wouldn't cook. So that meant she and Dad took Gil, Beth and I out to dinner. Most of the time it was to Bob's Big Boy or Sizzler. After dinner was party time. Saturday night, more parties. I always showed up with my buddies. They smoked pot; I stuck to a case of beer. Those whispers I heard on the soccer field, I also heard at parties, "Oh, Rick and his crew are here, we gotta stay." I honestly felt like royalty, like I ran the party and ran the school.

Those times were great, but after I broke up with Shelley, I really lived the single life. A staple of mine was music. I was always the one to drive so I would pick up buddies and we would head to the park. And what would follow us every time? Girls, beers and our guitars. Much like most crazy guys, we formed our own group and even managed to play a few gigs. Our band played at some parties, typically whichever party had the most buzz. The nights we knew we were playing, the minutes before we went on was a scene from Saturday Night Fever. Our hair had to be done perfectly without one strand out of place. And naturally we were dressed to kill. We would play for half an hour and then start trolling for girls. We'd start at one party, hit two or three more and keep going around until we found the wife for the night. Late after the parties were done, there was always a food run, mostly to places like Jack in the Box or Pup and Taco. Fast food at 2 a.m. couldn't be beat. During soccer games, which I still played on weekends, I used to get such a kick out of recapping the night before with some of the guys and planning where to go that night.

Sunday was surfing. Well I surfed; the other guys just drank and partied. Our spot was lifeguard tower 15 at Zuma Beach. It had the perfect set of waves most of the time. When we decided to go elsewhere, it was Malibu or Leo Carillo or county line in Ventura. We could have written our own version of Surfing USA. If it was an extended three day or holiday weekend, we'd head up to El Capitan or Gaviota State Beach. The gang was my type of crowd, surf and soccer crowd. We'd find a place to camp on the beach and just party all night. When we got tired of surfing, it was motorcycle riding. One night, everyone got stoned, decided to ditch the bikes and ride cows. One guy fell off his cow and landed in a fresh heap of cow dung, covered head to toe. We laughed so hard we cried. But even that didn't stop us. We got cleaned up, guitars and beer came out, and so did the girls. The Eagles could be heard playing on someone's stereo. If not them, it was the Doobie Brothers, David Bowie, or Ricky Nelson. Other favorites were Bread, Ted Nugent, Linda Ronstadt, Kansas, Foreigner, Steeley Dan, and Jackson Brown. Naturally so were the Rolling Stones and the Beach Boys. Any time I look back on a great time or a great party, I can always associate those moments with the music that always seemed to be a part of those great times. It was just the best time of my life.

The best time of my life took a detour after one of those long weekend beach parties with my buddies. We were twenty-year-old guys having the time of our lives. We spent Memorial weekend 1980 at Gaviota. It was a typical night for us, partying, guitars, and music. On the 2nd day I met a beautiful brunette named Tara. Right away we had that eye contact, her in that tiny bikini looking so hot. I knew I was going to spend the night with her, which happened the next night after everyone else had left to go home. Somehow, it was just the two of us. We had a very intimate weekend capped off by a very intimate one-nighter. At least I thought it was going to be a one-nighter. Tara and I did exchange numbers the next day before I drove home in the 110 degree heat. I remember it like it was yesterday. The AC unit was not working at home so I decided to jump in the pool. I could hear the phone ring, it was Tara. She wanted to get together.

"Already?" I thought. So I made something up, "I can't tonight but I'll call you." Which, like most guys my age, I never did.

Six months later I received a very random letter in the mail. It was from Tara, who informed me in the body of the letter, that she was having twins. And then the dagger: they were mine. Right away I called her to verify and she asked me to meet her at the park to chat. Once she emerged out of her blue Volkswagen, I saw the big belly. Then and only then did it hit me. She was absolutely six months pregnant. She proceeded to tell me that I was the father and that she didn't want a penny from me. Naturally I was terrified. I couldn't eat or sleep. What were Mom and Dad going to say? I could hear the words that they told me so many times, "You better wear a rubber, every time."

That one time I didn't. A couple of days after our meeting at the park, I finally let Dad in on my trouble, telling him that I got someone pregnant and she was having twins. To my surprise, he wasn't fuming mad, just disappointed for a bit. His words, "We better call Bernie."

Bernie Steinberg was the family attorney. He took care of all of the legal matters for us, and so we consulted him for this as well.

After we told Mom and talked to Bernie, we decided that after the birth we would request a DNA test. Mom and Dad were there at the hospital when the twins were born. In her typical Mom way, Mom said, "Rick, don't even bother with the test. They're yours." She knew. So did I.

Despite Tara saying she didn't want anything from me, we worked out a plan for child support so my kids, that I didn't get a hand in raising, would at least get my financial obligations. I'll never forget my Dad's words of wisdom, "That has to be the most expensive can of beer you've ever had."

I look back on those days after Shelley as one big party, but hard work nonetheless. It was a time that involved Dad, Gil and me building hot rods, skateboarding down hills and riding ice blocks down Reseda Boulevard making drivers turn their heads wondering what the heck we were doing. There were neighborhood block parties, motorcycle riding, lots of sports, beaches, girls, surfing, skiing, fishing, great music and great times. You see, I was on top of the world.

Even still, Shelley seemed to be the one thing I was never able to completely shake. All those emotions came back to me in the parking lot that day, and I had to put them aside and leave them in the past. Forgetting my Dad's cigarettes after being physically and emotionally drained, Shelley and I parted ways and I headed home. That night, I just couldn't go out. By eight o'clock, I was in my bed sawing logs. I awoke to the blaring ring of the phone. It was my cousin Kevin. He was having a party at his frat house. I didn't know it at that moment, but that frat party was about to introduce me to my future.

4
UH-OH

"Rick, its Kevin, wake up."

"Kev, stop calling man, I'm tired and I don't want to go anywhere."

"Suck it up. Big party time at the house. You gotta stop by."

"Dude, I'm going motorcycle riding in the morning. I need a good night's sleep."

"Come on man, it's our welcome back party. School doesn't start for another week. You can meet some of the pledges and get a look at the new chicks on campus this semester."

"Kev, I appreciate the invite but I just wouldn't feel right. I'm not even a student. Plus, I'm exhausted. I worked 60 hours this week."

"So what? You're my cousin. You get an honorary bid to our fraternity and an invite to any and every party we have. You could almost walk here. And besides, if you say no, I'm gonna keep calling until you get your butt over here."

"Fine. I'll be there in 45 minutes."

There were many reasons I didn't go to college. One of them was the fact that I wanted to come and go as I pleased. Parties were one thing. Parties where you have to be fake and "fire the pistol" at every wannabe pledge? Not for me. But I guess if I was going to make an appearance, I had to do it right. So I put on my nice collared shirt, nice slacks and boots, fixed my hair and jumped in the truck to drive to this shin dig, which really was just a mile away. After all, it was free beer and free food.

I walked through the door a few minutes past ten. Kevin came over to me with a Michelob. At least he had that right.

"Hey Rick, glad you could make it. What do you think?"

"It looks like a scene from Animal House," I said.

"I know, isn't it great? It's gonna bring in all the best pledges and attract all the hot girls."

"Kevin, you know that every frat house in the nation that saw Animal House is gonna have toga parties like this. I'll be going now."

"Come on Rick, give it a chance."

"Fine, I'll be over on the couch with my beer and a bowl of popcorn."

I don't think I would ever consider myself a snob but this scene just wasn't for me. It was a bunch of guys trying to impress girls with how fast they could down a stein of beer, yelling at the top of their lungs and stuffing their faces with hoagies. What did these girls see in these guys? As I was finishing my beer, all I could think about was how much longer I wanted to be here. I'd scanned the room for possibilities of girls I could go talk to, nothing that wowed me. Nothing that made me want to get off this pretty comfortable yet pretty skuzzy couch. I will say this, I was the only guy here dressed nice. If I couldn't pick up a chick here with every other guy dressed in a toga, I might as well have gone home and… Wait a minute. Who was that walking through the door?

"Kev, who is that?"

"That's Danica. She's dating one of the brothers."

"No. Not her, her friend."

"Don't know. Never seen her before."

"Well this party just got a lot better. Look at the way she moves. She's dancing while she strides through the room."

"Shame on you, Rick. I see the way you're looking at her."

"You're just jealous I saw her first. Just look at that body in those red leather pants. I'll be back."

I know for a fact that Cat Scratch Fever by Ted Nugent was playing on the stereo. But that faded away as I moved closer to her. Before I spoke, I detected an alluring scent of flowers and then that million-dollar smile as I introduced myself.

"Hi there, what's your name?"

"I'm Rachel Parker, are you with the fraternity?"

"Hi Rachel. I'm Rick Martinez, nice to meet you. I'm not with this house. I'm actually not even a student here. Are you?"

"No, my friend's boyfriend is a member here and they asked if I wanted to come along. I had to tell my parents we were going to a movie. They would never approve of me going to a fraternity party."

"Well Rachel I'm glad you came. I wasn't having any fun at all and was almost ready to leave. Can I get you something to drink?"

"I assume they don't have any wine, what about a wine cooler?"

"I think I can find one for you."

As I made my way to the kitchen, every other step I was looking back to see if she was still looking at me, which to my delight she was. Rachel was tall, had dark wavy hair and had on a white blouse with tight red leather pants. And although her face was so angelic, I had a tough time moving away from her legs and butt in those leather pants. She was not only the most beautiful woman in the room, but she may have been the most beautiful woman I have ever laid eyes on. In my mind, I wanted to play this cool and be Mr. Wonderful, but at the same time there was something inside of me that kept my attention on only her. So I brought her back the wine cooler, to which she thanked me, and then we proceeded to carry on a few minutes of small talk. Rachel was living with her parents in Thousand Oaks, which was about 20 minutes from my parents' house. She then asked why I didn't have a drink in my hand, which was out of the ordinary for me. I guess I was so interested in every word that came out of her that I completely forgot all about me.

Twenty minutes went by and I decided it was time to go. But not before I got Rachel's phone number and asked her to come motorcycle riding with my buddy and I tomorrow. She accepted, although she warned me that she had never ridden a motorcycle before. I told her I would teach her how in the morning and that I would pick her up around 9am. I thanked her for the chance to meet her, drove home and went to sleep. The next morning, I jumped out of my bed as if I were lying on a spring. I showered, got ready and was downstairs having breakfast with mom by about 7:30am. Dad was already up and in the garage working on his truck.

"Mijo, what are you doing up this early on a Saturday?"

"You remember mom? Jim is coming over and we are going motorcycle riding today."

"Oh, that's right. Mijo, please be careful and come back in one piece. And don't get too crazy out there."

"Don't worry mom. Besides, I met a girl last night at Kevin's party. Her name is Rachel and she is coming with us."

"What!? Oh mijo, why would you want to take a girl motorcycle riding on a first date? And what's Jim gonna do on this date. He's just going to be a third wheel."

At that point I was realizing that maybe I hadn't thought this whole day through too well. What if she wouldn't like Jim? What if she got hurt motorcycle riding? What if she and I wanted to be alone and Jim is there? Why didn't I ask her to dinner tonight instead of riding all day? So I made something up to mom.

"Mom, at least I'll know right away if she can keep up with my world."

"Yeah but Rick, what are her parents going to say about motorcycle riding?"

"Mom, I'm not meeting her parents today. She's going to be outside her house at 9am when I pick her up."

"Oh no, Rick, we taught you better than that. You are going to meet her parents first. Please mijo, it's the right thing to do."

"Ok, mom, I'll do it."

Jim arrived at the house at 8:15. He had just enough time to use the bathroom and steal a piece of bacon that mom had made. We then loaded the bikes in the truck bed. I had to take out my surfboard and tool box to make room for the them. I then told Jim we were going to pick up Rachel. He did not like the idea of inviting any girl motorcycle riding. I just told him, "Wait till you see her, you'll understand." Besides, Jim had no choice. I was driving and he could ride his bike up ahead in the desert while we shared the four-wheeler. Plus, I was really looking forward to seeing Rachel, the sooner the better. We arrived at her parents' house at 9am on the button. Rachel was waiting outside as she promised. I parked in the driveway and exited the truck.

"Good morning, Rachel!"

"Good would have been at eleven. I can't remember the last time I was up so early on a Saturday. Who's the guy with the funny looking hair?"

"Oh, that's my buddy, Jim. He's gonna tag along with us today."

"My parents want to meet you. Can you come inside for a minute?"

"Yeah, that's probably a good idea."

I noticed that she lived in a nice house, in a very nice neighborhood. At that moment, I became a little nervous to meet her parents. To no surprise, they were at the front door waiting for me. Their faces had this look of concern and disdain. Rachel then began.

"Rick, I want you to meet my parents. Mom, Dad, this is Rick. We met last night at the movies." I was actually a little impressed. She was able to tell her parents a story and even I believed it. So I smiled, and with my best foot forward, I extended my hand.

"Hello Mr. and Mrs. Parker, it's nice to meet you."

"Rick, please call me Walter or Wally, how do you do?"

Her dad gave me a firm hand shake and an honest smile. He had to be well over six-feet tall, bearded face but with a very cheerful disposition. Her mother's name was Elfrieda. Barely five feet, heavy and looking at me with disapproval. She was very abrupt when she stated,

"Rick, whose idea was it to go motorcycle riding?"

So I scrambled up the best answer I could think of.

"Mrs. Parker, I realize it's not the traditional "dinner and a movie" type of first date, but I had already made plans to go riding and Rachel seemed to like the idea." Oh and then I added, "Plus we both saw a movie last night. I didn't think she would want to see a movie two nights in a row." Rachel winked at me with an impressed and somewhat approving smile.

"So where are you taking our Rachel?" Walter questioned.

"Up to Indian Dunes, just passed Santa Clarita."

Her mom, Elfrieda, threw in one more snarling remark, "Make sure she is back by dark."

Rachel detected that I was getting a little impatient so she said goodbye to her parents as she guided me out the door and to the truck. As we got in the truck, Rachel mentioned how happy she was that I remembered we supposedly met at the movies last night. Jim, from the back seat, introduced himself and assured Rachel that he wouldn't get in the way. As we got on the freeway, I turned on the radio and sure enough, the Eagles' "Take it Easy" was playing. And to my pleasant surprise, she asked if she could turn it up. Jim patted me on the back as if to say how lucky I was to find someone who loves the Eagles as much as I do. It was an hour drive to the desert, but it went by very fast because of the nice and easy conversation between us. Jim even managed to be somewhat quiet, allowing us to get to know each other. Once we parked and unloaded the truck, Jim took the bike and was about to take off when Rachel chimed in.

"How come I don't get to ride that?"

To which I replied with a grin, "I thought you had never ridden a motorcycle before."

5
INFATUATION

Waking up the next morning, I reached for the phone. Wait a minute. Was I going to call Rachel less than 24 hours after I had just seen her? No, I had to wait. I had to give it at least a couple days. I didn't want her to know just how much I liked her. Then I started racking my brain, replaying yesterday moment by moment. Did I open the door for her? Did she like the conversation? Was it a great first date in her mind? Would she want me to call as soon as possible? This was all new for me. The last thing I had ever expected was to put this much thought into one date, after the fact. So I tried to go back to sleep. Perhaps if I slept another hour or so I could wake up to my normal self. The me who would have asked myself why I didn't get lucky and then head to the beach. Except it wasn't working. When I closed my eyes, I saw Rachel. When I opened my eyes, I thought about our date. Was this what girls did after every first date?

The smell of food got me out of bed for sure. Mom was cooking huevos and papas and I was betting there was some homemade salsa to go with it. As I headed downstairs I was determined to keep my date buried down deep inside. I was going to go about my day and not think about her.

"So Rick, how was your date?"

"Geez mom, no 'good morning?' No 'how did you sleep?' No 'what would you like for breakfast?'"

"Mijo, I already know the answers to those questions. Besides, I really want to know if this girl truly enjoyed motorcycle riding on a first date."

"Mom, I gotta say, I had a great time. Rachel is incredible."

"Good mijo. How were here parents?"

"Her dad was very nice and warm. Her mom gave me the once over. Not sure about her yet."

"Rick, that's what I would have done. Don't worry, I'm sure she'll be calling over here as much as the other girls used to."

You see, that's what I was used to. I'd go out with a girl, we'd have our "fun," I'd take her home and she would be the one to call the next day. And I would have to decide if I would take the call.

After a great breakfast, Dad had me help him with the sprinkler system out in the back yard. He was in his typical stubborn mood. There was some cussing and some throwing of the tools followed by some ordering me around. Gotta love Sundays with Dad. Even though I knew the answers, I had to ask, "Dad, if you hate doing all the repairs in the back yard, why did you build the new house? Why didn't we just stay in the old house? It had a great pool." His quick response, "Because your mother wanted a bigger house. She doesn't swim well anyway so we felt we didn't need a pool anymore."

About six months ago, Dad had built this castle of a house a few blocks away from the house we grew up in. I didn't understand it really. Gil and Beth were out of the house already so mom and dad get a bigger house? You would think it would be the other way around. Personally, I think Dad was just bored and wanted something to do. It was everything he wanted on the outside and everything Mom wanted on the inside. Everything was custom made, from the cabinets to the bathrooms to the mini bar. If you asked Mom she would say that he built it for her. She was right.

After a full day of sprinklers with dad, I couldn't wait any longer. I called Rachel after dinner. To my relief, she was very excited to hear from me. We replayed the date together and she mentioned that she wanted to drive the motorcycle the next time, since I didn't let her despite her begging. We must have talked for an hour, although it felt like ten minutes. The conversation was just so easy with Rachel. Her voice was so soft, almost as soft as her skin. I loved her laugh. I loved the way she would try to tease me. I loved that she seemed to listen to my every word, just as I was listening to her every word. We said good night, although I wasn't ready to hang up the phone. I called her the next night and we did it again. We had an hour conversation on the phone every night that week. We also planned a day trip on the upcoming Saturday to go skiing with some of her friends. To my surprise, she wasn't a good snow skier. She was a great snow skier. I had a tough time keeping up with her, which I absolutely loved. I had to ask, "How did you get to become such a good skier?"

She replied, "My parents go up to a little town near Yosemite at least a half dozen times every winter. I learned how to ski there way back as a little girl."

"No kidding. We go to Mammoth all the time. Never have been to Yosemite."

"Well if you like Mammoth, you will love Oakhurst. That's the town my parents stay in. It's only a half hour from Yosemite's gate. They have always talked about buying a place up there. One of these days, I bet they take the plunge."

At that moment I just couldn't get enough of everything about her. Not only was this beautiful woman kicking my butt up and down the ski slopes, but she had captivated me to the point where I forgot about everything and everyone around. I know it had only been a week but it was like I was addicted to her. Her aura, her mannerisms, Rachel became a drug to me that I just had to have. I wanted the drive back home to last a week and a half. She was so innocent, so warm, so unassuming that I just never wanted to leave her side. Her friends dropped me off at home and Rachel walked me to the door. Talk about new. And I knew her friends were watching. Hell, maybe my parents were watching. I didn't care. I planted a big, long kiss on her red lips. We could hear her friends go crazy. Big applauses and cat calls, maybe even a standing ovation. I think one of them gave us a perfect 10 as if they were judging an Olympic event. As I went inside, it was Dad's turn to ask me how my date went. "Dad, I'm gonna marry her."

"What? Honey, get in here and listen to what your son just said."

"Mom, Dad, I'm gonna marry Rachel someday."

They weren't jumping for joy or reprimanding me. They just looked at each other and then Mom requested, "Well I guess you better bring her by for dinner soon so I can give HER the once over."

The proceeding week was much like the last. Sure I was working the typical long hours, but all I was thinking about was Rachel. Then at night, of course, we would spend hours on the phone chatting about everything and nothing at the same time. I extended the invite for dinner on Friday night, which was big for my family. Not only was

I bringing a girl over for a family dinner, but it was on Friday night, the night Mom never cooked. Gil was going to be there. So was Beth. Rachel gladly accepted saying she was looking forward to meeting the family.

I've never been the nervous type, but from the moment work ended that upcoming Friday, I was a basket case. The fact that I was apprehensive about Rachel meeting the family, that told me my feelings for her were not only true but on a different level than any girl in the past. I showered, got ready and went downstairs to find Gil and Beth already there. Beth had that look in her eye. She was determined to embarrass me or find something wrong with Rachel. I can still hear Gil's voice say, "OK chump, let's see who this girl is." Whenever Gil said the word chump, he always emphasized the letter "P." This was no exception. And then the doorbell rang. Rachel was here.

I gave her a kiss, asked her how her day went and took her by the hand into the living room.

"Mom, Dad, Gil, Beth, this is Rachel. Rachel this is everybody."

After the introductions, I gave her a ten-minute grand tour of the house. She was in love with this new house. The size, the décor, the marble in the bathrooms, she loved it all. Every room we went to, I joked how I would love to have my way with her in that room. Naturally it made her blush a little, but I sort of wanted to take her temperature on the idea. Just kind of see where she was at with fooling around.

It wasn't a formal evening you might see in a movie. Nobody was really dressed up, except for Rachel. She arrived in a stunning red dress, not too short, not too long. I think Gil's mouth dropped to the floor at one point. We all sat down and had the typical "get to know you" conversation. My family had a way of asking those questions in a job interview sort of way. Clearly, they were friendly and welcoming when getting to know Rachel. But they also had an interest in how she was answering each question, almost studying her every move. After a few more minutes, Mom led us to the kitchen.

"Rachel, I hope you're hungry. I think I made enough for a weekend's worth of meals."

As I mentioned before, Mom was the best cook. Especially when it came to Mexican food. I have to give her credit. She made a traditional American meal. Chicken and scalloped potatoes, corn on the cob and fresh dinner rolls. I think Mom calculated that Rachel would probably like this meal more than any Mexican dish for fear that she may have never had it before.

Mom then continued, "Rachel, that is a lovely dress."

"Thank you, it was on sale at the mall last night. To be honest, I bought four of them. I couldn't decide what to wear tonight. I guess I'll be returning the other three."

"Oh really, what stores do you like to shop at?" Mom was now excited.

"Whatever stores have the best sales. I'm not able to spend much money. Although I did see a shirt that would have been perfect for Rick."

"Well Armand, it looks like I found a new shopping partner." As she turned to Dad, both he and my brother had lost some interest in the conversation.

After dinner, we spent another half an hour in the living room visiting. Rachel then explained she had to leave because she had committed to going to church with her family early the next morning. I could tell that Mom was impressed by that as well. As she got up to leave, everyone took their turns giving Rachel hugs and saying how nice it was to meet her and that they hoped to see her again soon. Even Beth seemed very receptive and warm towards her. I walked her out to her car, which was actually her Dad's car. We probably spent 45 minutes kissing and messing around a little. I told her how bad I wished no one was in the house, that we could continue this upstairs. More blushing on her part, but hey, at least she wasn't declining. I asked if I could see her tomorrow. Her response, "You better come see me."

As I walked back in the house, everyone was still in the living room watching TV. To my surprise, Dad was the first to comment.

"She's a nice girl, Rick, don't screw it up."

That's as nice of a comment that I could have expected from Dad. Beth continued, "Yeah Rick, she's seems nice. Hopefully she doesn't screw it up."

Kind of an odd comment from Beth but, ok, I'll take it. Gil's turn.

"Yeah chump, we'll have to go to the White Horse Inn sometime and double date."

Gil had been seriously dating the same girl for some time now. The White Horse Inn was one of the nicest restaurants in town. Plus, they had been known to serve wine without asking for an ID, so it was a good idea to bring my eighteen-year-old girlfriend to this nice place. Mom then asked the question I was waiting for.

"So, Rick, you still think you're going to marry this one?"

"Mom, I know it."

6
PARKERS

The next month or so was great with Rachel. We'd get together often during the week. It would be anything from going out to dinner or just hanging out listening to music. On the weekends, we'd go to the beach. I'd take her to the drive-in movie theater or even something as simple as a trip to Farrell's, the local ice cream parlor. We laughed constantly. She would try to tell me that Barry Manilow was better than Ricky Nelson or that Johnny Lee was better than George Strait. She believed it, but also would say it just to get under my skin a little. I had to set her right, "No one is better than George Strait." It didn't matter where we were, we would even enjoy getting in my truck taking a drive. Naturally, we had to get a little creative when we wanted to be alone for that "ring-a-ding-ding" time. After all, her parents were always there and Rachel always felt a little uncomfortable when we went to my parents' house. When we weren't together, I would always call to say good night. One night, I called a little too late.

"Hi Mrs. Parker, may I speak to Rachel please?"

"You know Rick, it's a little late for a phone call, don't you think?" Elfrieda snapped back.

"Oh, I'm sorry about that. I just wanted to say good night to your daughter, if I may?"

"Not tonight but perhaps you'd like to come over for dinner tomorrow night so the family knows why Rachel hasn't been around much lately."

"Why sure, I would love to. What should I bring?"

"Nothing Rick, just make sure you are here promptly at 6:30. See you then."

The entire next day I thought about going shopping for a new suit or at least a new tie and shirt. I thought about asking Rachel what I should be on the look-out for. In the end I decided that, while I would charm Rachel's family, I'm just going to be myself and show them who I am. Nothing more and nothing less. Well, nothing less than a sharp dressed man with a bouquet for Elfrieda. I realized right away that she was the one who I had to impress. She was the one who Rachel tried to impress. She was the one who ran the household.

I had to give Elfreida some credit. One sunset evening over a bottle of wine at the beach, Rachel shared her family story with me. This was right after I had told Rachel about Tara and having Kaylee and Jack. I explained my situation which she accepted without questions, thankfully. Then she proceeded to explain hers. Wally worked the night shift for a janitorial company while Elfrieda stayed home with the kids. In fact, that was how Elfreida and Wally had met. She was working at a grocery store, which happened to be a client of Wally's janitorial company. At the time they met, Wally had been married to the kids' biological mother, Dottie. Rachel continued that she didn't remember everything, just that her dad and Elfreida had an affair for months. Rachel was four years old when they made it official. Her sister, Lindy, was six and her brother, Adam, was barely two. Wally left Dottie and married Elfreida. A year later, Dottie decided to basically give up her kids. According to Rachel, her mother thought the kids would have a better life with Wally and his new wife. Elfreida then put her foot down the way only a strong German woman could, "Shame on you, Dottie. Just remember this, once you give these kids up, you'll never get them back." Rachel said that she only saw her mother a couple more times before Dottie decided to run away to the Midwest with a man. Rachel had never met him and she only remembered her mother referring to him as Brother Scarborough. Before I could finish my question, Rachel quickly responded, "Yep, a man of the cloth."

Naturally, on my drive over to Wally and Elfreida's for dinner that night, I was playing that conversation in my mind over and over. I couldn't believe how different Rachel's upbringing was than mine. I couldn't believe how blasé she had been about it. But most of all I wanted to make sure not to say anything that could lead to a story from Rachel's childhood. I did not wear a jacket but did have a tie, nice shirt and nicely polished shoes on. And yes, I did have a bouquet of lilies for Rachel's mother. I knocked on the door.

Rachel answered and gave me a big kiss. Even I pulled away after a few seconds for fear that her parents might see us. She eased my worry by telling me that her mom was preparing dinner and her dad was in the shower. As she led me into the living room, we stopped in the kitchen to give her mom the lilies, to which she graciously thanked me. In the living room, I met her brother, Adam, who was still in high school. Adam was a shy kid who still had bad acne all over his face and probably lacked a little in the self-esteem department. He was still very friendly to me as we watched the Lakers game on TV. A few minutes later her dad walked into the living room, sat down and asked who was winning. Wally was a sports fan much like myself and enjoyed his Los Angeles Lakers. Well he enjoyed them since Magic Johnson was drafted by L.A. the year prior. Adam, Wally and I watched Magic lead a few fast breaks. Rachel helped her mom in the kitchen for a few minutes before Elfreida yelled, "Boys, wash up, dinner time."

As I found my way to my seat at the dinner table, there were many things that I noticed. First, there was classical music playing on the record player. I hadn't heard classical music since my 6th grade music class. I also noticed that the silverware was as shiny as could be. The napkins were soft, silky cloth and folded neatly. The glasses, already filled with water, were made of crystal, and everything was perfectly placed. I wondered if this was an every meal occurrence in the Parker household. I guess I was expecting filet mignon or rack of lamb presented to us by a servant or a maid. What we got was chicken parmesan with garlic bread and veggies. At least it was good. According to Adam, it was better this time around than it was the night before. And before I had the chance to guess, Wally sort of poked fun at Elfreida that the best thing she made was leftovers. Well that, and reservations. Wally got the glare that I half expected to get from her as Rachel's new beau. After all, I was the reason she hadn't spent much time at home. I asked where Lindy was. Rachel mentioned that Lindy and her boyfriend, Chad, went out to dinner and would be home later. And just as I was settling in making myself at home, the Parkers interrogation began. Actually Wally and Adam sat back, giving each other a wink in amusement. They seemed to get a kick out of me squirming in my seat as Elfreida took full control of the evening.

"So Rick, did you know that our Rachel once had a bright future as a dancer and she hasn't mentioned it at all since you came into the picture?"

"No, I didn't Elfreida, this is the first time I've heard about. Rachel, I knew you liked to dance. I didn't know you were thinking about doing it full time."

With an embarrassed look, Rachel replied, "It's no big deal. As a little girl I loved ballet and as I grew up it sort of became more of a chore than a passion."

It didn't take long for Elfreida to jump back in. "But Rachel you were such a talented dancer. Your instructors all said you could have danced on Broadway. Why did we spend all that money on that school in San Francisco if you were just going to throw it away?"

Thank God Elfreida didn't say she threw it away for me.

"Mom, the bottom line is that dancing is fun but nothing I want to do long term. I'm thankful for all the time and effort we all spent on it but I'm happy it's over. I just want to dance for fun without all the responsibility."

Elfreida paused for a minute and then changed quickly to another subject.

"Wally, did you know that on more than one occasion your daughter has come home from a date with Rick and there has been wine on her breath?"

Her father devilishly replied, "No kidding?! What kind was it?"

"Actually daddy, it has been both red wine and white zinfandel." Rachel said as she gave her mom that 'Haha, dad doesn't care' grin. They laughed along with Adam and I. Elfrieda? Not so much. There was some more small talk amongst everyone at the table. I was beginning to like this family more than I had anticipated. I actually loved that they were middle class. They weren't nearly as rich as they wanted other people to believe them to be. The Parkers very much had a champagne taste with a beer budget. There's nothing wrong with that in my mind. We were all having a good time until Rachel's mom once again put a stranglehold on the evening.

"Listen Rick, we don't mind you taking Rachel out. You seem to really like her and she seems to really like you, but what would be so wrong about the two of you hanging out here from time to time?"

Just when I was about to throw something quick and witty out at her, I had to pause in thought. She was right. We didn't have to go out constantly. We did have a lot of fun wherever we went. Why not spend time at her house once in a while. So I reached out to Elfrieda, "I can understand and respect that. I do sometimes forget that Rachel is only eighteen and, like me, still lives at home." Then I decided to turn on the charm. "Just to let you and Wally know, I do care for your daughter very much. My intentions are very good and very respectable. I love spending time with Rachel, and with your permission, would love to keep spending time with her. Since we met, there hasn't been a day that has gone by when I didn't think about her. I love her." I must have had my chest puffed out at this point as if to ask her mom 'what do you have to say to that?'

"That was good." Then Wally corrected himself, "I mean, that is good. After all, we just want our Rachel to be happy."

I knew I had them at that point. I guess I shouldn't say I had them, but I knew they were coming around. Plus, I knew at some point I had to tell them about Kaylee and Jack. That would really be the true test. There was no way they would take it as well as Rachel did. No way would Elfreida take it well at all. We finished dessert and spent some more time in the living room. Adam left to go out with his friends. Wally, still working the graveyard shift, got dressed and went to work. I was left alone to watch TV for a bit as Rachel helped her mom clean the dishes. Part of me was leaning over to hear what they might be saying. However, the other part of me was thinking about tonight with me and Rachel in a much bigger light. Her situation with dancing sounded very similar to my situation with soccer. We had passion for it at one time but in the end, it was more about fun than anything else. Now that I understood her mom just wanted to see more of Rachel and I around the house, this relationship just kicked up into a serious one. Where exactly was this going?

Then Elfreida came in the living room, said good night to both of us, and went to bed, leaving Rachel and I to hang out in the living room. We felt closer than ever before and would have attacked each other on the couch except for the fact that Lindy and her boyfriend Chad could walk in at any minute. So we did what any couple would do. We chatted, all night. I don't know where the words came from but they just sort of slipped out, "I'm getting my own place soon. What do you say about moving in with me?"

Rachel, very much in shock, replied, "What?! I can't do that! Are you serious?!"

"Yeah I'm serious. I love you and want to be with you all the time."

"Rick, I love you too, but the only way I would move in with you would be if we got married."

"Ok, then tell your parents we're getting married. Then we could live together."

I realize that at this point I wasn't making a whole lot of sense. I didn't even have my own place yet, and here I was asking an eighteen-year-old girl, still living at home, to tell her parents that we were going to get married just because I wanted her to move him with me. Right after Rachel said ok she would do it, her sister Lindy and Chad walked in, which ended our deep conversation until another time. Rachel and I stayed up talking until around 4 a.m. As I left, Wally walked in. He patted me on the back then invited me back for Easter Brunch. I replied, "Sure, why not?"

A few hours of sleep later, I was headed back to Rachel's house feeling good about dinner the night before. However, when I pulled into their driveway, a funny feeling came over me. I shrugged it off, blaming it on my lack of sleep. I rang the doorbell, and when Rachel answered, she gave me a big kiss. Then, as she led me into the living room, her parents and Lindy were there waiting for me. I wished them all a Happy Easter and asked where we were headed for brunch. Naturally it was Elfreida with the response, but not quite what I had expected.

"Well, Rick, Rachel tells us you two had a long conversation last night. Between that and dinner last night, Wally and I realize how much you love Rachel. She tells us you want to get married."

I hadn't forgotten what Rachel and I talked about. But no way in hell did I think she was going to tell her family right away that we were going to move in and get married. So clearly I was caught off guard when I responded, "We do? I mean, we do."

Well Elfreida jumped up as high as a heavy, 5-foot-tall woman could possibly jump. She let out a big yell, "Rick, welcome to the family! We are so happy!" She, Wally and Lindy all gave Rachel and me a big group hug. I looked at Rachel, sort of happy, sort of stunned. Within a matter of seconds we moved into the kitchen where Rachel, Lindy and Elfreida began laying out the plans for the wedding. The date, the dresses, the flowers, you know, the typical girl stuff. Wally practically lit up a cigar and put his arm around me as if I was already his son-in-law. I knew I had one thing left I had to say.

"Listen, there is just one thing I gotta say first. Wally, Elfreida, before I marry your daughter, I feel it's only right that I tell you I have twins with another woman. They were just born but my relationship with their mother was before I met Rachel and has since ended. I guess what I'm saying is that I'm a father of a girl and a boy. Their names are Kaylee and Jack."

The room became still like a fishing pole gets before a big hit. At that moment, all eyes were on Elfreida. Rachel, Wally and Lindy directed their attention to her, as did I. We were all waiting for her response with baited breath.

"So?! Rick, as long as you are good to Rachel and are a good father to your kids now, and a great father to your future children with Rachel, that's all Wally and I care about."

No way could I ever have predicted that from Rachel's mom. So it was my turn to let out a big yell, "Right on!"

Wally then stepped in, "Listen, we have plenty of time to plan this shindig. Let's go have brunch. Then we can talk about the details."

Before we left, I used their bathroom. As I was washing my hands, I stared at the kid in the mirror, aging before my very eyes. Then, I whispered, "Rick, you son of a bitch, you're getting married." What were Mom and Dad going to say?

7
SHOCK

Easter Brunch seemed very nice. Not that I could tell you where we went. The food was damn good. Not that I could tell you what I ate. Rachel and her family started planning the wedding. Not that I could tell you what they had in mind. You see, I was still a little stunned about what had gone on at the Parker household. I was engaged, yet had not purchased a ring. I was going to get married, yet had not gotten down on one knee to propose. Wedding bells would be ringing, much louder than the alarms that were sounding off in my head. Could I even stop this locomotive that was the Parker women? 11 a.m. suddenly became 3 p.m. and it was time for Rachel and I to head to my house and spring this news on my Mom and Dad and the family. I'm sure Rachel was blabbing like crazy in my truck on the way. But again, I had no idea what she said. I couldn't even tell you what was on the radio. You see, there were two things swimming in my head. One, do I dare talk to Rachel and see if we can somehow slow down this wedding stuff? After all, I hadn't officially asked her and never dreamed that it would go this way. Two, which one of the family would strongly object first?

Before I pulled in to the driveway, I stopped a block early and pulled over to the side.

"Rachel, what are we doing?"

"What? We're telling your parents about us getting married."

"I know but how did we get here?"

"What do you mean? You told me that I should tell my parents we were getting married so that we could live together."

"Yes I know, but we haven't mentioned moving in once. Since I got to your parents' house this morning, it's been nothing but talk about getting married."

"Rick, what's wrong with that? I'm excited. Aren't you excited?"

"Well sort of. I guess I'm still getting used to the idea. Rachel, this is all happening so fast."

"Be honest Rick, do you want to marry me?"

"Well yes…"

"Then it's settled. Come on, let's tell Armand and Helen."

And I thought I had some more to get off my chest but Rachel gave me that million-dollar smile that I just couldn't resist. So I put my truck in gear and pulled into my parents' driveway.

"Rachel, one last thing. Please let me be the one to tell them."

"Ok, but don't take too long. I may burst if you delay it at all."

Walking in the door, I started to get very nervous. Rachel and I went into the kitchen and saw no one. So we shared a glass of water and waited. I felt like I was in the principal's office sitting and wondering what punishment I had coming to me. And almost simultaneously, dad came in from the garage and mom came down the stairs.

"Oh mijo, when did you get here?

"Happy Easter Ma, Rachel and I have been here for a few minutes. Happy Easter Dad," and we gave them both hugs.

"Happy Easter to you both. What's wrong?" You couldn't get anything past dad.

"What do you mean dad?"

"Well, when I hugged you, you seemed tense. When I hugged Rachel, she was shaking."

"Well, yeah dad, we have some news."

And then just when I was about to blurt it out, mom went first.

"Oh Rick, you got Rachel pregnant, didn't you?"

"What?! No Ma, not that." I looked over to Rachel and she asked, "Do I look pregnant?"

Then Mom, Dad and Rachel went on for a couple minutes about the way she looked and how what she was wearing didn't make her look pregnant at all. I lost control of the conversation and didn't know how to interrupt cleverly. So it was my turn to blurt it out.

"No, Mom, Dad, we're engaged." To which my dad responded in only the way he could.

"To do what?"

"Dad, we're getting married."

I didn't emphasize it. I didn't sound confident. I sort of just said it, almost to test the waters and see just what that might do to the room. I could see Dad's smirk drop a little. Mom was speechless. Rachel looked at me. Then she looked at them. Her gigantic smile lessened a bit. I could tell she was waiting for me to say something. Or perhaps waiting for them to say something. It was only a few seconds of silence but it felt like an hour. Then Dad ventured a safe question.

"So, when did this happen?"

Rachel felt it was her turn to pipe up.

"I guess it sort of happened this morning."

I could see the shock of my dad now.

"You guess? What do you mean you guess? Did you flip a coin this morning and when it turned up tails, you say, hey, why not get engaged?"

And just when Rachel and I were about to walk away with our tails between our legs, I heard him laugh.

"Congratulations to you both. Rachel, welcome to the family."

Mom was still, sitting at the dinner table, looking like she had no idea what to say. That is until dad nudged her.

"Honey, aren't you going to say anything to your son?"

"Oh yeah, congratulations."

I could tell she only sort of meant it.

"Listen Rick, do me a favor and take Rachel home. Your dad and I want to talk to you." She paused and thought for a moment and came up with the first excuse that came to her mind, "about the arrangements and other wedding stuff." Rachel bought it.

"Sure Rick, I'm pretty exhausted. Besides, I know my mom and sister have many, many things they want to go over."

I knew what my mom meant. I knew they were going to lay into me. So I drove as fast as I could, dropped Rachel off, and raced back home. To no surprise, when I pulled in the driveway this time, I saw my brother's and sister's car. Ok, so they're going to gang up on me. I guess I should have seen that coming. Part of me was more nervous than a couple hours ago. But part of me was ready. Or so I thought. As I walked in the door, I could almost hear the ringing of the bell ringside at a boxing match. To no surprise, Beth started first.

42

"Rick, are you out of your mind!? You can't marry her. You don't even know her. What are you thinking?"

Then my brother Gil chimed in.

"Yeah chump, I don't know. Why do you even want to get married right now anyways? You're only twenty-one."

"Guys, I know you are a little shocked but just give it a chance."

That comment did not sit well with Beth. "Rick, give what a chance? Clearly you aren't thinking straight. Don't marry her just because she puts out."

"Beth, I don't want to hear that, especially not from my sister."

"Ok, then I'll really say what we are all thinking. She is only eighteen and she only wants the family and the money. She hasn't worked a day in her life. She has no direction. She wants to get out on her own and find herself. And she just found herself a guy with more means than most at twenty-one. Listen to what I'm saying. DO NOT MARRY HER."

Then it got silent again. At this point, I felt like I was in a television show. I felt that my family was ganging up on me trying to find any and every reason to stop me from marrying Rachel. Just then, I started to find the courage to fight back until my mom hit me with this:

"Mijo, have you even thought about what you just agreed to? You aren't just buying a new surfboard that you may or may not keep around long term. This is marriage. Vows. Lifetime commitment. Are you really ready to give up your childhood and begin life as a man?"

That shook me inside. I was only twenty-one. I was still living at home. I didn't like what they were saying, but was it because of the words they were using or perhaps because of the way they were saying them? So while they were throwing things at me right and left, I really tried to think about what I wanted. What was really best for me? What did my parents want me to do? Then I realized I was tired of wondering what my parents or what my family thought. I was ready to be my own man. I was ready to begin life as an adult. Then I put my foot down:

"Listen guys, you don't have to agree with me. You don't have to like this or even like Rachel. But you know what, this is my decision and you better get used to it. Rachel and I are getting married and we are going to live life together."

I thought I had really slammed the gauntlet in that kitchen. Then my dad floored me:

"Son, what the hell do you know about building a life with someone, sharing life with someone and doing this, 'til death do us part?' Just think about this, by marrying this girl, you are giving up on all other girls for the rest of your life. Do me one favor, talk to Rachel and see if you both even want the same things in life."

I thought to myself, "I don't even know what I want. How do I know what she wants?"

8
PREPARATION

Planning a wedding can be a very magical time. A man and woman can decide on many things together. After all, they are preparing for the most important day of their lives, the day that is supposed to start their lives together. Some details may not be as big. Some may take a lot of time and there is a lot going back and forth on the decision. Rachel would have been fun to do all these things with. However, Rachel went to her mom and sister with these details. Part of me was completely fine with that, but there was a part of me that wanted at least some input. For example, the day I was going to look at tuxedos, Lindy told me what my groomsmen and I were going to wear. I asked if we could have chicken kiev as a meal option. Elfreida informed me that we were having salmon or filet. Ok, I can handle that. Then there was the day I went to Rachel and wanted to discuss the song list for the reception.

Her words, "Don't worry about that. My Uncle Shawn is taking care of it.

"I see, but what if I wanted to help with that or at least hear the bands we were deciding on?"

"No, Rick. He is singing at the wedding."

"What? Come on Rachel. Can your Uncle Shawn even sing? Can he sing country, rock and R&B?"

"Rick, he knows what he is doing. Trust me. I'll take care of the details."

"Uh, by yourself? Rachel, how are we, actually, let me rephrase. How are you going to get everything into place? And how are you/we gonna pay for all this?"

"Well, I am going to sit down tonight with my parents and discuss that with them. No need to worry."

So I walked away sort of satisfied. Rachel says her parents were going to take care of this. I was ok with that. I know this sounds a little girly, but I did want a nice wedding. Not too many people, but enough to have a party to remember. I was hoping to play my guitar at the reception, sing a song to Rachel, something romantic, something she would never forget. I just wasn't sure about this Uncle Shawn. Rachel had never even mentioned him in all the times we talked about my passion for music. I was trying not to stress out about the details at all, and especially about how quickly this big day was coming. I had enough stress with the fact that my family was not exactly on board with the wedding. I tried talking with Rachel about their concerns: the timing of it all, the logistics of starting our life together, where we were going to live. All she kept saying to me was that everything would work itself out. Sometimes, she actually convinced me, but sometimes the uneasy feeling stayed with me. Sometimes I had to force myself into thinking I was ready for this lifelong commitment. Deep down, I just wasn't 100% sure. "I'm sure that's pretty normal" was another thing I kept telling myself.

Then there was the battle within about money and selflessness. I thought I made a pretty good living and was saving a lot of money by living at home. I could live on my own in a nice one or two-bedroom apartment. I could save up some more money and start traveling a bit. Perhaps even start a band for real and give the music thing one serious attempt. Marrying Rachel and starting a life with her would pretty much give up all of those possible dreams. Marrying Rachel would start the list of what ifs in my life. Number one on that list of "what ifs" is the woman factor. At twenty-one, was I really ready to wake up next to one woman every single day until I died? No way could I share those thoughts and fears with my family. The "I told you so's" would pile up like the dirty clothes in my room. Before I let these doubts pile up even higher, I decided to take a few beers in the garage, throw some darts and blow off some steam that way, until it was time to pass out, feeling nothing at all.

"Rick! Wake up please! We have to talk!" a startling wake-up call from my bride to be.

"Rachel, what time is it?"

"It's after 8, get up!"

"Come on, I didn't get to bed till sometime after 3 a.m. Let me sleep a little longer."

Her response, panicked, "Rick, we have no money for the wedding."

"What do you mean? I thought your parents were taking care of all of this."

"I thought so too." Rachel was in tears by now and I have no idea how to calm her down.

"They said we can have a small wedding but nowhere near what we want. Twenty to thirty people at the most."

"Rachel, if it's a small wedding, that's ok with me. In five to ten years, if we could do it right and do it bigger, we'll do it then. The most important thing is that we love each other and that we get married."

At this time, I could hear a voice in my head disagreeing with me wholeheartedly. Did I really believe what I was saying? Where were these words coming from? This was my way out. We could postpone the wedding, do it right when we could and take it slow. And right when these words start making their way up to my mouth...

"Rick, what if we ask your parents to help with the wedding?"

"HELP pay for the wedding? Or pay for the wedding?"

"Well, they have the money don't they? I mean look at this house. Surely they can afford it."

"I don't know, Rachel. They were planning to travel now that us kids are all out of the house. I'm just not sure."

"Rick, can you do it for me? Please?"

There was that face, those eyes, that smile. For some reason, I found myself not being able to say no to this woman. I wondered if she knew she had this power over me. I had the same realization I did after our snow skiing date. I was addicted to her like a dangerous drug. This sweet, innocent girl had this power over me at eighteen years old. Sad, but true, I guess.

"Ok Rachel," I said very, very reluctantly. "I'll see what they say but please do not get your hopes up."

I loved Rachel, but I'd be lying if I said this wasn't a red flag. There was just something that wasn't right about her asking my parents to pay for this. I did want a nice wedding, a wedding that people would remember. I wanted a day that Rachel and I would remember. But is it really ok to ask mom and dad to pay for this wedding? I decided to clear my mind and headed down to the beach. Surf was up, or so I heard, and

I had to catch some waves and get away from things for a few hours. On my way back to the house, I collected my thoughts one last time and decided that a big wedding would be nice, and perhaps mom and dad would be happy to throw one. I'd just say it would be like the big parties we used to have, except this one wouldn't be at home and there might be a few more people than usual.

Later that afternoon, I finally sat down with mom and dad and laid it all on the table for them.

"Listen, Mom, Dad, I'm not sure how to say this so I'm just going to throw it out there. Rachel has her heart set on a big wedding, but her parents won't be able to pay for a lot, so I was hoping you might be able to take control and pay for it."

I could see mom getting very excited and ready to scream with joy for a big party, but dad was not quite as thrilled.

"I don't understand, Rick. Don't Rachel's parents understand that it's the responsibility of the bride's family to foot the bill for a wedding and reception? We would be happy to pitch in, but I think Rachel should be having this conversation with her mom and dad."

"Dad, I agree with you, but it sounds like she already has talked with them and they let her know how much they can contribute, and it doesn't sound like much. Anything you and mom can do would be a big help."

My mom couldn't control herself any longer.

"Mijo, what do you want?"

"Well Ma, part of me doesn't care. We could always do this years down the road, but I kind of do want a nice wedding. And I know how happy this would make Rachel."

"Then your father and I will be glad to throw you and Rachel a nice wedding."

I was shocked it was that easy. Well I thought it was, even when my dad threw in a caveat.

"Listen Rick, we are more than happy to do this but we will have to put a limit on the number of guests, and please see if her parents can help out with some of the costs."

"Mom, Dad, I can't thank you enough. This will be the best wedding present we could ever ask for."

I called Rachel and told her the great news right away. After all, we had a wedding to plan. And when we found out the only place in the area in our price range was available on July 26, we found out that this wedding was happening in less than 3 months. We all took a deep breath to collect ourselves as if to say, "Well, let's do it." Rachel still insisted that her uncle sing at the wedding, but I got to pick most of the music, which was the one aspect I really wanted a lot of say in. Lucky for us, things really seemed to fall into place. Invitations went out and we got our responses quickly. Mom and Dad kept the guest list to a max of 150 people. Some may say that's a big wedding, but for us Mexicans, that's barely bigger than a family barbeque. I got the tuxes. With both of our mothers' help, Rachel got the dresses. In my mind, I was thinking this was just too easy. Was this a sign saying this is right, or was this a sign saying this is too easy? I got my answer the night before the wedding.

We had our rehearsal dinner at the White Horse Inn. Just family and the bridal party made the evening very intimate. Well, intimate for a while. After dinner, my buddies pretty much kidnapped me and let me know I had no choice on how the evening was going to go. I barely got out one question to Rachel before I was dragged out of there.

"Hey Rachel, what time do you want me there?"

"Well if the wedding is at 5p.m. please try to be there no later than 4."

"No problem, just please don't be late."

I guess you could say that it wasn't your typical Vegas bachelor party. Just me and a group of guys bar hopping around the valley. All they kept telling me was to say goodbye to all these establishments. They insisted that bars would be the last place a husband would be after work and on the weekends. I partly agreed with them. I understood certain changes may be in store now that I am thinking for two and not just myself. But I sure wasn't going to change completely just because there was going to be a wedding band on my finger. Plus, Rachel was only eighteen years old. Clearly she had some living left to do. Clearly, nights out with her friends and with me are still doable. We were getting married. We weren't retiring or applying for social security.

Each of these thoughts, along with many others of the big day details came and went in my head with each shot of liquor and each contest of beer guzzling. Somehow, I was always in each competition. My friends made sure of it. The last stop of the night was a bar called Webber's. Not that I remember how much I had to drink, but I do know that half way through my last beer, a song came on the jukebox. Mechelle by the Beatles. Right then and there I asked a buddy to take me home. I guess I'd had enough.

Waking up that hot summer day, July the 26th, let me tell you it was a minor miracle I wasn't hung over. Just feeling a little off from sweating out the alcohol while passed out on the floor in front of the air conditioner in my underwear. My buddy and his girlfriend stopped by to make sure I was alright and to see if I needed anything before I headed to the country club. Then I started singing for some reason, Mechelle my Belle. Again that song by the Beatles. Mechelle. For some reason, Mechelle became Shelley and it began a moment of day dreaming. What was Shelley doing? How was she? Did she even know I was getting married? Was she married? Boom! It hit me that I had to see her. So I took off in my truck, not quite sure what was going to happen next. At that pay phone, I all but pleaded that Shelley meet me for lunch. I needed to hear what she thought of me getting married. Would she be happy? Would she try to talk me out of it? Did I want her to talk me out of it? Did she still love me? Did I still love her?

You know how a movie has a big confrontation? Perhaps it's at a house. Perhaps it's at the top of a mountain or some monumental place. For me, Rick Martinez, perhaps my big moment in life would be at a Denny's. I was sitting at a booth when she walked over to join me. She walked with purpose. She walked with cause. She walked like a model on a runway. And her first word to me was...

"Well..."

"Shelley, I'm not going to beat around the bush. I want to marry you. I'm marrying the wrong girl." Immediately she started crying.

"Why would I walk down the aisle when I'm still in love with you?"

"Whoa, whoa, Rick. Slow down. You're getting married?!"

"Well the invitations say I'm scheduled to in a few hours, but that depends on you."

"Rick, I guess deep down I probably still love you, but I just can't."

"Shelley, I understand me just springing this on you is unfair, but I still love you. We can do this."

"Shame on you, Rick! Yes, this is unfair to me. But this is also unfair to her. No way am I letting you do this. You wanna call off the wedding? I can't stop you from that. But there is no way in hell I am going to be the reason."

That statement took Shelley a few minutes to get out through her tears and emotions. And before I could respond…

"Goodbye Rick. Please do the right thing."

And she ran out of the restaurant, still crying.

What seemed like an entire sunrise and sunset of a conversation, it really only took an hour. I must have sat in that booth for another hour, just myself and my thoughts. How could I marry Rachel now? Finally, I got back into my truck and raced to the apartment, our new apartment. The one Rachel and I were going to start our life in. All I could think about was whether or not I should call off the wedding. Once I got there, I struggled to put on my tux. Then, a knock at the door. Another confrontation. A different confrontation. Mom and Dad.

"What the hell is the matter with you?"

"Dad, what do you mean?"

"Shelley just left our house in tears. She told me what went down at Denny's. How can you do this? If you take off, what do you think that will do to Rachel?"

"Dad, I love Shelley. I got to do what I got to do." Now it was mom's turn. I expected her to be in tears as well but she was solid as a rock.

"Rick, can you really leave Rachel at the altar?"

"Mom, I don't like the idea but I don't think I can go through with it."

"Oh mijo, you're going to break her heart."

"So what am I supposed to do? Just marry Rachel because the invitation says I have to?"

"Mijo, I know you still love Shelley but you need to let her go. Finish getting ready. We'll see you over at the club. Be there at 4."

And that was that. There was no doubt in their mind I had to get married. But the reasoning puzzled me. If I was truly having second thoughts, why would they force me to do this? I understand it would be unfair to Rachel not to show up, but would it be fair to her if I married her knowing that I was in love with another woman? And make no mistake, I was still in love with Shelley. Perhaps I was in love with two women at the same time. After a few minutes of the back and forth in my head, I decided that it was time to finish getting dressed and head to the country club. I guess I was still marrying Rachel, and I guess it was because it was the right thing to do. I figured I should keep that sentiment out of the vows.

9
COMMENCEMENT

I made the commitment. My parents expected me to do it. Those were the thoughts in my head. Not anything like "I love her so much. I can't live without her." Looking back, it didn't take a genius to see that I was going into this Holy Matrimony with all the wrong thoughts and all the wrong answers. I guess my instincts, you know the ones of being a man, they just took over and almost pushed me into my truck and to the country club. I was getting married whether I liked it or not. I'll say this though, had the roles been reversed, I wished she would have cancelled or postponed it. But my mindset was let's get this over with.

I arrived at the club right on time and saw the pomp and circumstance of the event unfolding before my very eyes. People were all dressed up in nice suits and dresses. I swear the temperature was getting hotter and hotter. At that point, I decided to track down an employee of the country club. I simply asked her to put some sort of security guard at the front to make sure no uninvited guests would crash this wedding. Hey, I may not be the smartest human alive but I knew there was a slight possibility of Shelley barging her way into the room during the ceremony. Although deep down, part of me was wishing she would come and break this up. One, it might give me a reason to not go through with the ceremony. But two, and maybe just a bit self-indulging, I was sort of hoping to see what would happen if Shelley and Rachel met face to face. Would they fight for me? I know it's sick, but hey, that was one of the many, many things that popped in my mind in this whirlwind July afternoon.

After the club stationed someone at the front, with a very quick pace I made my way to the dressing room, hoping none of the guests along the way would ask me how I was feeling. I put my best fake smile on and tried not to make eye contact with anyone. Someone handed me a beer as I got into the room. By myself for a few moments, I tried to collect my thoughts. That beer was gone in a minute or two at the most, and I needed another one. What I really needed was time. Time I didn't have. And right when I was about to get up and get the hell out of there, the rest of the wedding party arrived. My brother, the groomsmen, mom and dad. I could see the happy yet concerned face my mom had. She knew what I was thinking. And leave it to her to do just the right thing. She handed me another beer. Mom could tell how nervous I was. My brother took it upon himself to invite another ex to the wedding and reminded me that I didn't have to go through with it, joking in his brotherly way. He had no idea what went on earlier. Dad then floored me.

"You sure you wanna do this?" Now he asks me this. Now he realizes, just a few minutes before I walk out to the altar. Where was this before? And at this point all I could say was, "Yeah, dad, I guess I have to. Rachel expects to see me at the altar."

Rachel. I seriously hadn't even thought about her all day. All I was going through was about me. It had nothing to do with what she was doing or how she was feeling or how her life was about to change with any decision I was about to make. Trying to keep that in mind, it was very hard to relax. Nerves started to run throughout my body. Perhaps it was the ice cold beer in the midst of that stuffy room. A buddy brought a surfboard into the room, asked if we should go surfing instead of getting married. Everyone else seemed to stop by the room, Elfreida and Lindy, then Wally and Adam. They were all congratulating me as if the ceremony was over. They were also telling me how beautiful Rachel looked, which somehow brought me back to, "What if Shelley shows up?" It was settled, I was in love with Shelley AND Rachel, at the same time. I don't care if it was right or wrong, it was the truth. Then my best man Barney said, "Rick, let's get this sonofabitch on the road."

Like perfect timing I got to the altar as the music started. Like a movie director, I took in everything that was going on. Watching the procession and the bridesmaids walking down the aisle, I became even more afraid, even more nervous. Everyone looked so happy, so sure, so much like a perfect picture. If they only knew what was going on inside my mind. The conflict inside me, the back and forth, the what-ifs, the thought of, "Am I really doing the right thing?" or "What is the right thing?" I had always heard about life flashing before someone's eyes before they died. That was going on at the moment I saw Rachel walking down the aisle. Here comes the bride. Gut check time. Now or never.

The preacher looked at me almost as if he was checking to make sure I was ok. Perhaps God sent him a message that I was unsure at this moment. There was no doubt how beautiful Rachel looked walking down the aisle. Like the guests, she also seemed so happy, so calm, so sure. In her face, in her eyes, there was no doubt what she wanted. And she had absolutely no idea what had gone on earlier that day. She was probably having her make-up done while I was professing my love to another woman. Once Rachel arrived, I took her hand and prayed she didn't feel it tremble the way the rest of my body was trembling. This eighteen year old girl trusted me with the rest of her life. Even without my meeting with Shelley, that was a lot to ask of a twenty —one year old guy. Me, her and the rest of our lives. Big gulp before the preacher begins. Even with the veil still over Rachel's face, I saw her beauty, and was hoping my thoughts and fears weren't transparent.

"Dearly beloved, we are gathered here…"

I was looking at Gil, looking at my buddies, trying to find a sign from them. Trying to find some sort of answer or comfort. I guess I was still looking for a way out. Perhaps a reason not to do this that even Rachel could agree on. All my guys kept giving me a thumbs up, but I still wasn't convinced. 150 people were as happy as could be, including the bride, but there was one who was scared to death. I'm sure the preacher was conducting a heartfelt sermon and a lovely ceremony. Then the words, the vows, or in my mind, the lifetime contract.

"Rachel, do you take Rick…" and so on and so forth. No hesitation, no fear. She was ready, happy, and nothing was going to stop her. A resounding I Do. Then my turn.

"Rick, do you take Rachel…" And this next minute or two seemed like an eternity to me. It truly was the turning point of my life. Could I say the words? Could I convince Rachel? Our families? Could I convince God? Could I convince me? Shelley, Rachel, the rest of the women in my past. All these thoughts racing through my mind, and then, uh oh, my legs became jello. My head was dizzy and I got light headed. Timber!

The next thing I remember was waking up at the base of the first row of pews, sitting on my butt with my head between my legs. And there was everybody. Mom and Dad, Gil and Beth. And there was that smile, Rachel's smile, who softly stated,

"Rick, you take as much time as you need to feel better and then we'll continue."

Sold. I was now ready to go through with it. I got the strength back in my legs, got my blood back to my head. I repeated the vows from the preacher, said I do and that was that. I was married and my wife's name was Rachel Martinez. Did I feel 100% satisfied with everything and hear the music you hear in those romantic movies? Not exactly, but I did feel a heck of a lot better than I did an hour before. Let's party! Let's drink. But Elfrieda reminded us that we had pictures outside. Damn it! I thought the wedding stuff was over. We took what must have been 400 pictures. I really can't complain. It really was a pretty quick wedding, must have been no more than 20 minutes, although part of it felt like 10 years. Now, let's party!

Luckily for us, we didn't have to go anywhere, as the reception was at the same place as the ceremony. I really had to hand it to my parents for shelling out the money for this. And I had to hand it to Rachel, Elfrieda and Lindy. Not that I noticed all the little touches of color and other girly stuff, but the place looked great. Everyone still seemed happy, and I think for the first time all day, I cracked a big, real smile. Then the band introduced Rachel and I for the first time as husband and wife and I got chills up and down my spine. They magnified, but in a good way, as they started playing "Feels So Right" by Alabama. That was the one part that I made sure of. This first dance was incredible. It felt amazing as the lyrics were sung, "Just hold me close and love me. Tell me it won't end. MMMMMMMMMM! Feels so right." At that moment, I felt like king of the mountain. I felt all our guests admiring the new married couple. You could see all the joy in our families' faces. You could see the happiness in my new bride's face, and that truly made me happy. I figured if I could make someone that happy, if I could have someone look at me the way Rachel did on the happiest day of her life, I must have done something right.

After the first dance, the traditional dances proceeded. Father-daughter and mother-son dance. Towards the end of my dance with mom, she whispered the words she always did when I was kid. "No matter how old you get mijo, you'll always be my baby." And then she added, "Be good to one another."

The guests sat down for dinner and I still can't remember what we ate. However, during the meal, it was Rachel's Uncle Shawn's turn to sing. I don't know why I was so uneasy about this. Rachel said that he was going to sing no matter what. So he got up there and with a booming voice he welcomed everyone to the event. He congratulated us and said all the right things. Then he began to sing "Edelweiss" from The Sound of Music. What a performance, very touching and very beautiful, especially when accompanied by the piano player. At the end of the night, I stood at the bar, beer in hand, and for the first time in a few weeks, I felt good, comfortable, and confident. I was ready to be the husband Rachel deserved. We spent that night at a simple Holiday Inn. There was no real romance that night, just sex to say we had sex on our wedding night. To tell you the truth, we were both just too exhausted. It didn't take long for both of us to fall asleep.

We woke up the next day and went to mom and dad's house to get the cash from the dollar dance. It was another scorcher of a day, 105 plus degrees. Rachel and I were both ready to get the hell out of the San Fernando Valley and up to Yosemite for our honeymoon. We were scheduled to stay 6 nights at the Ahwahnee Hotel in the heart of Yosemite's valley. Getting there sometime Sunday evening, we checked in, had a very romantic dinner and then it was time for the romance. Rachel bought a very sexy negligee. Naturally I was ready for it all. Again and again. Even after we went to sleep, Rachel was so cute. Every hour she would get up and check her makeup to make sure nothing was out of place. She wanted to stay perfect in my eyes.

The first morning we woke up, had breakfast and lounged by the pool all day drinking bloody marys. We needed that day to just relax and unwind. The days that followed were set for sightseeing through this beautiful area. This truly was God's country. The waterfalls, the deer, the giant redwood pine trees. I wish we had remembered to bring a camera. One day in particular as Rachel was hiking and admiring the beautiful scenery, she slipped, fell and skinned her knees. The rest of the week I teased her that she got too drunk one night and fell down. That inside joke went on for a long time.

Although we were supposed to stay an entire week, I convinced Rachel to leave Thursday. I wanted to get home early and spend a couple days at the beach for some surfing and R&R. What can I say, the beach, the board, the waves, that was truly my second home. On our way back, we stopped in that little town where Rachel had learned to snow ski in Oakhurst. I remembered her saying that her parents would probably move up here to retire. I looked around and thought, "Hell, I could see myself here with her, raising a family someday."

We then spent a very wonderful and perfect Friday, Saturday and Sunday together. Sunday night, Rachel and I were lying in our apartment bedroom. I asked her, which I probably should have asked her months before, "So, what do you think you want to do now?"

"I don't know Rick, I'm pretty exhausted. I don't think I can go another round in bed right now."

For the first time, I didn't mean sex. "No, silly, I mean what do you want to do this week, next week, for the rest of your life?"

"It's funny you should ask that Rick…"

Then the phone rang, which was a bit surprising at almost 10 p.m. that night. It was the boss, dad to be specific.

"Rick, you're home right? We need you for a job. It starts tomorrow."

"Dad, come on. I had planned on another week off."

"Rick, I need you." Something Dad had never said to me before. "Besides it's good money. We'll be working at this site for six months. Plus, if all goes well, I might be able to get my hands on the Penfield house. If you're interested, that is."

Talk about life starting out on the right foot. Six months of good money leading to moving into my old house and it would be all mine. Well all mine and all Rachel's. So I hung up the phone and was about to tell Rachel about the great job and great pay coming my way when she continued her original thought regarding what she wanted to do next.

"Perhaps I can get a nose job."

10
NEWLYWEDS

Married life was great. I would wake up in the morning and Rachel would always be there in bed next to me to greet me with a good morning kiss. You see, my wife, my sweetheart, my baby or whatever pet names we called each other was awake with me in the morning. That's just a nice refreshing way to start the day. Then after a nice breakfast, as I'd walk out the door to another hard day's work, Rachel was there to say goodbye, give me a kiss and give me something sweet to think about over the course of my work day. And all of those little things to think about, all the wonderful ways my wife has made things better in my life, it just made me want to run to a pay phone to call her up and tell her I'm thinking of her. Then after that hard day's work late in the afternoon I knew that I would have somebody there waiting for me to greet me at our front door. Rachel would give me a big hug and a big kiss and was genuinely interested in how my day was and would tell me she thought about me all day long. And on the really good days, Rachel had the place all clean. She did the dishes, she cleaned the bathroom, she vacuumed and just maybe she had dinner ready when I got home. Or at the very least, dinner was cooking and almost ready. Of course there was always that time when we would just sit down on the couch to watch TV and just relax. After dinner it was always nice to have this time with somebody like Rachel because we would always go for nice little walk around the block. Sometimes we'd go out for a drink to throw some darts and blow off a little steam. There were also times when we'd stay home and play board games or just listen to music and unwind. Rachel and I had such a good time getting used to living together as husband and wife. Her learning about my little mannerisms and me learning about her little quirks was new and fun and exciting. Then, the best part was night time when we were ready to go to bed and of course it was time for that ring-a-ding-ding. Or as Rachel would put it, tender love and care time. Married life suited me perfectly.

Married life was also trying at times. It was also difficult, and frustrating. It was tough for me to compromise even when I knew I was right, even when I didn't want to give in. You see, when I would wake up in the morning, Rachel was always there. And if I ever wanted the morning to myself? That just wasn't possible. Rachel was always home while I was getting ready for work. During breakfast she always seemed to be talking to me about how she planned to go shopping, which was not what I wanted on my mind over the course of the day. The last thing I wanted to be thinking about was how much money I needed to make to satisfy Rachel's shopping habit. It also seemed that when I got to work, all anyone wanted to talk about was how married life was. Or how's the Mrs.? Or how's the old ball and chain? All I wanted to do was work yet someone was always there on the job teasing me about being whipped. No way I was whipped, was I? Then of course at the end of the day I might have wanted to go out for a drink during happy hour with some of the guys from work or perhaps some of my old buddies. However, I couldn't really do that at the drop of a hat because I was married and I had somebody that was waiting for me when I got home. Chances are, I was probably so exhausted from working a long day and I would want to just take off my shoes, kick my feet up, have a beer and just sit in silence. But I couldn't do that either because the place wasn't that clean and she didn't go shopping and dinner hadn't even been thought about yet. And it also couldn't happen because Rachel was always there. Always wanting to know about my day. When I'd say it was ok, her response, "Well was it a good day? Was it a bad day? Did you talk to anyone special?" You know, a million and one questions before I could barely get a word in edge wise. Then of course when I did have something to say and wanted to have a nice conversation, all I heard was how Rachel cleaned out the department stores with things we don't need. Money we didn't need to spend. She would ramble on about the gossip at the salon because she had to get her nails and hair done. She'd tell me about what her mom and dad did that day, the day before that and the day before that.

Once I got passed that and passed the dinner or whatever it was we ate, edible as it may or may not have been, I would love to sit down and watch the Dodgers. Perhaps watch a movie. Even pluck my guitar for a little bit. Anything to get my mind off of life and just be at ease. If I could just get through the evening and get to bed early, I would be so happy. Whether we had sex or not on those nights were the least of my worries because that seemed to be the one constant. I just wanted to have a few minutes of peace and quiet and get to bed at a decent hour because I knew Dad wanted me at the jobsite before sunrise. I tried to fall asleep after a couple of beers but it was nearly impossible because Rachel still hadn't stopped talking or she was sleeping like a rock and her snoring was louder than an alarm clock.

Yes, married life was great, but I wasn't prepared for how tough it would be. The funny thing is that nobody tried to tell me about any of this, or did they? Isn't there supposed to be some sort of manual? Aren't there some sort of instructions or some sort of work book? Were we properly prepared for the certain little things that would come up on a daily basis? I was supposed to have certain answers, certain tidbits, and certain ways to get around things. Shortcuts, cliffs notes of how married life is supposed to be, that's the way I got through high school. That's how I got through soccer. That's how I got through most of my relationships in the past. Then again, the women were always the ones who seemed to compromise. They always did what I wanted to do. As I learned in the first days and weeks of marriage, Rachel certainly was not about compromise. She was living on her own for the very first time and loving the freedom. It was always about what she wanted. And the funny thing is, as much as I disagreed with her, as much as I wanted her to do things certain ways and as much as I pleaded with her to think before she did things, it was of no consequence to her. Many, many times Rachel was on her own agenda. And it was always me who seemed to do the compromising.

No matter what, Rachel was a beautiful woman and no matter what, Rachel definitely loved me. Having said that, Rachel was not the best cook. Rachel was not the cleanest person I've ever met, even when she had eight hours to clean. Rachel was also not the most frugal person. Despite what she told my mom, I don't think she knew what an "on sale" sign looked like. It was all about style. All about how it looked on her. All about how she thought it would look on the weekends. It had nothing to do with a budget. As much as I tried to explain to her what a budget was and as much as I tried explaining to her what we could and could not afford, it did not stop her from finding a way to pay for it. In fact, she learned about credit cards from the saleswoman at JC Penneys. Once she found out that she didn't have to pay with cash or check, it was like the opening of the flood gates. She came home from a day of shopping with nine new accounts opened. No food was bought. Nothing but clothes. No necessities for around the house.

This was not the married life I had pictured with Rachel. I wanted her to have the same views about money and hard work that I had. She started out this marriage like gangbusters, gangbusters at the mall and all the stores, that is. And it all seemed to start when I said no to that nose job. Although I didn't say no, I just said not now. I wanted to start off with very little unnecessary expenses. Work hard, save up and get that house. That was my priority. And when I tried to explain that to Rachel and show her that this house was a good thing for us, her response was, "We have plenty of time for that. Let's enjoy life and be free." While that did make some sense, I didn't know her being free would be so expensive.

Once the work week was over and the weekends arrived, I would have loved to spend time at the beach like I used to. I would have loved to get together with the guys and play some music all night long. I would have loved to go anywhere fun. However, that didn't seem possible in those first weeks and months. There was always something to do. Actually there was always something Rachel didn't do or forgot to do or didn't do the right way. Laundry was never completely done. I never understood how Rachel could put a couple loads in the washing machine and then get lost in a magazine. She was more entrenched in an article about soft skin than putting the clothes in the dryer. She always left them in way too long and they'd get wrinkled, which wouldn't be so bad if she decided to throw some clothes on the ironing board once in a while. If she did get to all the clothes, it was only because she had new stuff in there from the department stores and was eager to wear something.

Cooking was another area where Rachel lacked some basic skills. Not that I was a gourmet chef, but I did take pride and joy and learned some of the tricks of the trade. It seemed that once a weekend I was on the phone with Mom asking her how to make this or how to cook that. I needed advice from the expert. She could always tell me just how much of this spice I needed or how long that needed to be in the oven. Mom sharing her family recipes and other suggestions was good for our meals, but it was also good to catch up with what was going on at my old home. It gave Mom time with me that she was used to when I was around. After all, the nest was empty, which was great for me and although she didn't see it, great for Mom and Dad. They could begin to travel and enjoy life after all those years raising Gil, Beth and I. And I wanted that for them, as long as I got the help I needed on dinners.

During one of the dinners I prepared on a normal Saturday night, Rachel abruptly mentioned the nose job again.

"Rick, I think it's time. I'm ready for a nose job."

"Rachel, we need to save up more money. We gotta get the house first. I don't want to be in this small apartment long term. Plus, you have not seen the house I grew up in. We could really make that our home and have fun."

"Well what if I get a job and help pay for it?"

I was wondering what type of work Rachel had in mind. I don't believe Rachel had worked a day in her life. But I bit my lip and asked, "Ok, what do you want to do?

"Well I think I can become a manicurist and do nails or perhaps an esthetician."

"I would say that's great, Rachel, but I assume you have to go to school for that. Which means more money to shell out. It's not a bad idea but I don't know that you can do both that and the nose job at this time."

"So what I am supposed to do Rick? Just sit at home and keep it cleaned all day? That's going to get boring pretty fast."

"Well if you are bored at home, then perhaps we can get you enrolled in a beauty school. But we gotta get this house first. I know if we can be a little more careful about our spending, we'll have enough for a down payment in a matter of a couple of months. Please Rachel, just be patient."

"So you're saying that I have no choice between now and then? You're saying that I can either get a nose job or go to beauty school but only after we get the house? That seems unfair to me."

"Rachel, look at it this way. We get the house in a couple months. After we move in, you can get a nose job. You can take the extra time to rest and recover. Once you do that, then we can get you into cosmetology school. A good school that will place you in a nice, upscale salon. What do you think?"

"I don't know Rick. It seems like a long time to wait for those things."

"Rachel, I'll make you a deal. After we get settled in the new house and while you are recovering from your nose job, I'll hire us a maid temporarily to help around the house. That way you can take your time and get ready for cosmetology school. Deal?"

"Rick, that's great. I can't tell you how lucky I am that you treat me like a princess. I love you so much."

Some negotiating on my part. I just committed to buying a house, paying for a nose job, getting a maid and enrolling Rachel in school. All of this was supposed to happen in the next year or so. Boy did I have my work cut out for me. But at least we could get the house first and at least Rachel seemed to be on board. As we cleared the table, I began to do the dishes. Rachel led me by the hand and whispered in my ear, "Leave them for now. I'll take care of you tonight and tomorrow I'll take care of the dishes." Now that's negotiating I could get behind.

The next morning, I woke up late, almost 11am. I can't remember the last time I slept in and slept so well. Guess I needed it. As I rolled over and expected to touch Rachel, I only felt her pillow. She wasn't there. Oh yeah, she said she would do the dishes. Maybe she would do the entire kitchen. I got dressed and headed into the living room but not before stopping in the kitchen to make myself a bowl of cereal. Except the kitchen was not cleaned. The dishes from the night before were not done. In fact, none of the dishes were done. And Rachel was nowhere to be found. I called over to Wally and Elfreida's house. They hadn't seen or heard from her. Lindy also didn't know where she was. Perhaps she went to get some food.

So I dove into the dishes and the kitchen for a good hour, scrubbing and washing and cleaning. I was almost done when Rachel walked in the door.

"Where did you go? I thought you were going to do the dishes."

"Yeah I thought about that but decided to go to the salon instead."

"Oh I see, you wanted to research beauty schools."

"No, I got my nails done. Mani and Pedi."

"Uh, Rachel, I thought we were going to monitor our spending more?"

"Oh come on Rick, it didn't cost that much."

"Ok, well can you at least help me with the rest of the kitchen?

"Oh Rick, I can't. It'll ruin my nails."

I couldn't help but think logically. Why didn't she clean the kitchen first and then go to the salon after? That is, if she really needed to get her nails done. I was ready to present that thought to her when she cut me off.

"Rick, I was talking to some of the ladies at the salon and they helped me come up with a great idea. You know how after the nose job, you were going to hire me a maid temporarily." Why did I get the feeling something bad was about to happen. "I think we should just hire a maid full time. That way I can have the nose job and when I'm in school, I won't have to worry about stuff getting done around the house. How does that sound?"

It sounded like this was Rachel's world and I was just living in it.

11
TUG-OF-WAR

There was a time back in my teens when I was playing soccer in Europe and I felt like I was on top of the world. However, I might have taken that feeling a step further now. It was the summer of 1984 and for those that lived in Los Angeles, 1984 reminds almost everyone of the Summer Olympics. Los Angeles was booming at that point and had recently surpassed Chicago as the second biggest city in United States. With all due respect to the Big Apple, Los Angeles was where "it" was at in the mid 1980s. Plain and simple, I was living life the way I wanted to live it in 1984. I was a few weeks shy of my 25th birthday. Rachel and I had been married for about three years and we had been settled in our house on Penfield for over a couple years now. In a way, I knew Rachel didn't love the house as much as I did. How could she? This was the house I grew up in. This was a great start in our lives.

I was still working for dad and we had been working on some big jobs in the Hollywood Hills, Beverly Hills, and Malibu. Building houses, swimming pools and guest houses for big-time Hollywood directors, athletes and financial gurus. Naturally this was good money for me. And to see some of their houses and to know that I was contributing to building their castles felt great. I was perhaps a little envious when looking at their houses and the neighborhoods, but not jealous. After all, at 25 years young, I really was living the life I wanted to.

As I left the job site one day and headed home, albeit in crazy traffic because of those Summer Olympics, I reflected on life. Where I had been, where I was and where I was going. You see, I was still having a little trouble saying "we," even after a few years of marriage. Chances are there was something like George Strait or the Eagles or the Beach

Boys cranking in my truck's cassette player. Things between Rachel and I seem to be going pretty well. She still loved her nose job. She had finished cosmetology school, and was working part-time at a nice salon up in Westlake Village, near where her parents lived. Although not for long. You see, Wally and Elfrieda had their house up for sale and were planning to move to Oakhurst like Rachel had always figured. They were going to retire in the mountains, which was fine by me. No way did I want them sticking their noses in places where they didn't belong. Although this did create a rift between Rachel and I. She wanted to move into that house, but there was no way could we afford a house in that area. At least not at this time. Even if Rachel was doing manicures and pedicures and assisting at the salon where she could to make some extra money, we still couldn't do it.

Rachel did seem to be very happy with the fact that she was making money on her own for the first time. But I could see the difference in the fact that she was actually earning money. And the fact that it wasn't just me that was bringing home the bread for the both of us, she seemed to gain some added independence. It truly changed her disposition. She was happier, more bubbly and just a few weeks shy of her 22nd birthday (Rachel's birthday is a couple weeks after mine), she seemed to turn the corner and took more pride in doing things for herself.

Don't get me wrong, this was still Rachel. She still liked the finer things in life. We seemed to go through housekeepers every few months either because they couldn't stay or Rachel just got in their way too often. I, too was making pretty good money. We were closer than ever with Mom and Dad, and with my brother and sister, too. I could still see Beth gritting her teeth anytime Rachel came along. She still felt that Rachel wanted the money as much as she wanted me. Even though Rachel and I weren't traveling much at all, we still found time to have our fun, whether it was going away for the weekend, going snow skiing in the winter or water skiing in the summer. We still spent a lot of time going to the beach of course, and going camping. But I was also learning that just hanging out at home and just having our alone time, that was ok too.

Almost home on that day I decided to stop at the store and pick up a case of beer and some food for dinner. I would relax, maybe jump in the pool. On the way home I also happened to pass mom and dad's house, their big castle that dad had built for mom a few years back. I still didn't understand why they needed all of the room when it was just the two of them. Gil, Beth and I were all on our own, with our own houses and building our own lives and families. But it still was a mansion to say the least. Everyone who drove by was envious. Everyone who lived on the street was jealous. I have to say, I absolutely pictured myself in a house like that twenty-five years from now. Maybe on the beach. Maybe in the mountains. Perhaps it was because it was located in the heart of everything, who knows, but I saw myself having the life that my dad had built for him and my mom. I felt that if I could work close to as hard as dad, that I could have that life someday. At 25, I felt that I laid a good foundation down for me and Rachel. We were able to put a decent amount of money away in savings and for kids down the line, just not yet.

I got home about six o'clock knowing that Rachel wasn't getting off work until eight or whenever the salon decided to close. It gave me some time to put together a light dinner for me and make sure that there was enough for her. I had no problem sitting down by myself, watching a game, having a couple of beers and just waiting for my beautiful wife to get home. As I finished my barbecued burgers and potato salad, I heard a big honking in the driveway. Not knowing who it could be, I went outside, turned the lights on only to see this brand spanking new green Camaro with Rachel in the driver's seat.

"Rachel, what the hell are you doing with this car?"

"Well I wanted to surprise you. A belated third anniversary gift for us. It's ours."

"What are you talking about Rachel? You just bought a brand-new car and didn't even discuss it with me?"

"I wanted to surprise you. Again, it's for us. Happy anniversary baby!"

"Rachel, this car had to cost $15,000, what the hell were you thinking?"

"I wanted something for the both of us. We have been working hard, putting money away. I wanted to reward us."

"You already have a car. I already have a car. Both are running and in good condition and they are paid for. We don't need this."

"Rick, I'm sorry that you are disappointed but the bottom line is you didn't have to give me permission. If you don't like it, tough. I'm keeping this Camaro. I like it."

"Rachel, I'm not trying to tell you what to do. If you truly want this car, I guess we'll work something out. I just don't know why you had to pay $15,000 for a new car when we have two cars in good condition and already paid off. But hey, just come inside, there's some leftover food ready for you."

"Rick, that is not the only surprise I have. I was talking with my sister and she thought might be a good idea if I decided to go to nursing school."

"Wait a minute, Rachel. We spent a lot of money for you to finish cosmetology school, we get you a pretty decent part-time job that pays you well, let's not forget the nose job and after a couple of years, you decide you want to do something else? Nursing?"

"Well, yeah, I can go to school. I'm surely not talking about medical school for years and thousands and thousand dollars, just something in the medical field. I can work at a hospital part-time. Besides, if I get into nursing, I can probably make more money than what I'm doing now working part-time at a salon."

"I just don't know what to say Rachel."

And I really didn't know. I guess I shouldn't have been too surprised. Just when I thought Rachel couldn't floor me again, she shows up with the Camaro and then wants to go to nursing school. I was just thinking on my way home how much I love my life; how well everyday life was going with Rachel. We were building a strong savings account. We were in our house. Everything seemed to be perfect. Then Rachel drops this on me. Needless to say the rest of the evening was not anything special. We'd passed each other in the hallway a few times. She could definitely tell how frustrated I was yet she seemed to ignore it because she was so happy with the car. She seemed hell-bent on becoming a nurse even though she had gone to beauty school. Apparently manicures and pedicures weren't cutting it.

So I decided to let it go. That was a Thursday night and I had to get up early Friday to get to the job in Malibu. After another day at work, I got home early. Rachel got off work early and we decided to sit down, have dinner and truly talk about this like two adults and really decide on what the best thing was for the both of us going forward in the near future.

"Rachel it doesn't bother me that you want to be a nurse and it doesn't bother me that Lindy somehow put this idea in your mind or talked you into it, because I know you like to do a lot of things. That's one of the great things I like about you. But do you really think that this is something that you want to do long-term even when we have kids?"

"I don't know if this is something I want to do long term. I just know that I want to do this right now. I like what I'm currently doing, but I think this is something I want to try, and when we do decide to have kids, I think this will be a good avenue for me and better prepare for being a mother."

"And that's fine, Rachel. And not to be selfish but what happens if you do become a nurse, when you are working all hours of the night, graveyard shifts, times that we could be spending together. You'll be working nights; I'll be working days, when will we see each other?"

"Rick, it will work it out I promise you. We will find a way to get through it. What do you say?"

"Look Rachel, I'm not going to say no to you now. I'm also not going to say yes to you either. Let it simmer for a couple of months, and after we have time to truly think about it for a while, get used to the idea, if you still want to go to nursing school and truly still see yourself as a nurse, then we can go for it."

"Rick, I want to do it now. I'm ready right now. I'll work at the salon for a few more weeks. Then I'm done."

"Rachel, isn't this is something we should decide together, unlike when you decided without me on the Camaro? You can't just decide on a career change without me. I'm not saying you need my permission but this is a decision made together as husband and wife."

"There's nothing more to discuss, Rick. This is what I want to do and it's final."

"You know what? Fine, do what you want, but just know this, from now on I'm going to do what I want to do."

I took my last beer, went to the room and slammed the door just loud enough for Rachel to feel the walls rattle. That was it. Something in my mind just changed right then and there. There was no point trying to reason with Rachel when she had her mind made up. I was going to start doing things without consulting her, without considering her. So I picked up the phone and started calling the guys, telling them to get over here and bring some beers. It was at this point when Rachel came in the room and asked who I was calling and what I was planning on doing. I told her I was planning on having a few people over for drinking beer and shooting pool. She knew she had no say in the matter. She requested that I keep it small and not party all night because she had to work early the next morning.

I politely said sure, but deep down I knew I didn't mean it. It was no longer time for compromising. What seemed like a matter of twenty minutes went by; I heard a knock at the door. Expecting to see about six faces, I was shocked when about thirty people showed up. And before I could invite them in, they stormed in and headed to the pool. It only took a few minutes for Rachel to interrupt and try to end the party. By then it was too late. Like an avalanche making its way down a hill, the party was well underway. In the wee hours of the morning, one of my buddies suggested we do this again tomorrow.

"What time?" I asked

"How about early, like six?"

"Sounds good to me."

Rachel woke me up the next morning asking me what the hell was going on.

"What do you mean?"

"Rick, there are people sneaking around to the back and setting up a stereo, some food and a keg. It's a few minutes past 6 a.m. You're gonna wake the neighbors."

I put my board shorts on, ran to the back, jumped in the pool and yelled, "Let's party!"

12
TIMING

The party that Saturday morning was well under way. Naturally, Rachel wasn't as excited as I was, even though she had to go to work. Before she left, she softly demanded that everyone be gone by the time she got home. I asked when that was. She replied "3 o'clock" as she was walking out the door. That request went in one ear and out the other. I raced to the back yard and rejoined the fun. I manned the barbecue and made sure the ice chest was full of ice and beer. There was plenty to eat for everyone. Before I knew it, the place was packed. On the stereo was pure rock and roll. The Eagles, David Bowie, Springsteen, you name it, it was blaring out of the speakers. It was turning out to be a great day.

It actually seemed like a high school reunion of some sort. Everybody there was catching up with one another. One thing I definitely noticed was the fact that we weren't sixteen years old anymore. We were twenty-five, and boy did the women sure look it. My high school years were flashing before my very eyes. The sexy women at sixteen certainly matured into their bodies. They looked better than ever. Each one of them came up to me and asked how things were going. They all remembered me, which I couldn't decide if that was a good thing or a bad thing. I was polite but stayed behind the barbecue. After all, I was the host and had to make sure everyone had a hot dog or burger. The women still flirted with me. I flirted back. I guess it was my nature.

By noon, 40 or 50 people were in the backyard. Even some of the neighbors came over. At first, they came over to ask us to keep the music down. But soon, after some convincing and some food and drink, they were all too happy and willing to join in on the fun. No one wanted to miss out on this party. It was nice to hear from the neighbors how happy they were that I bought the house. After all, I somewhat grew up with these people. This was my childhood house. One of them even went as far as saying that it was great that the house was owned by a Martinez once again. I couldn't have agreed with them more. What seemed like about an hour and a half turned into just past three that afternoon. Rachel strolled in just a couple minutes after. She was upset to say the least.

"Rick, what did I ask you for?"

"Rachel, relax. Everybody is having a good time. No one is doing anything wrong. Let's go back inside and we'll talk."

Although when we got inside there was only one thing that was on my mind. Get her into the bedroom, get undressed and have some fun. Perhaps that might take her mind off of things. At that point in my life, my libido was as high as ever. I wanted that sexual satisfaction two to three times a day, every day. I couldn't get enough. Sometimes Rachel would oblige. Sometimes she would refuse. In either case, it was easy to see that she was getting worn out. I just couldn't understand why she seemed to get upset when I wanted to fool around. Her response this time,

"Rick, you can't just take my clothes off, expect to get what you want and expect me to just forget about what's going on outside."

"Well, I know and I understand. But let's make up anyways."

She did, although I could see that Rachel was clearly not as into it as I was, but I got what I wanted. Afterwards, Rachel was the first to speak.

"Rick, we did it yesterday. We did it the day before that and the day before that. Can't you ever get enough? Is this all you want me for? Is this the only reason you married me?"

"Are you kidding? There are a dozen women out there in the backyard right now that I could have sex with. There are hundreds of women I had sex with in high school. If I truly wanted to just have sex with you, do you think I would've married you with all those options?"

Now I realize that this might not have been the best way to go about proving my point that I didn't marry Rachel just for sex. You see, this was the time we were just on completely different schedules and had completely different priorities. Since she started working at the hospital, I worked during the day, during the week. She'd work weeknights and on the weekends, I would work in the morning. I would be at the house either partying hard or at the beach, partying even harder. We were apart a lot those days. This was the new schedule since Rachel had become a nurse. I didn't want to stop her from working, especially if she liked it. But it was starting to take a toll on us. It was easy to see. Well at least easy for me to see.

"Rick, I don't understand why we can't have a nice weekend, just the two of us."

"We could Rachel. We could have that except you're not home half the time because of work. And then when you're not working, you're at the mall spending our money, still going to the salon getting done up and getting the gossip from the girls. I don't call that spending time together. I get that you want to work and I get that you enjoy work and I get that the hours are different, but I don't see you making any more of an attempt than me to spend time together."

"Rick, I don't want these people around. If you don't get rid of them, I'm going to my parents. I just want to relax at home. I just want to settle down, unwind a bit and take a nap. Maybe we can do something later tonight. Catch a movie, go out to dinner. Relax, just the two of us."

"That's the approach you always have when things don't go your way. Go to your parents and hang out. Don't you find it odd that when you lived there, you wanted to be away from home? Now you live apart from them and want to be there all the time. I'm having fun right now and I would love for you to come out and enjoy the party. Meet some people, catch up, just laugh and hang out. But if you want to leave, that's your prerogative. I'm not kicking people out. We're all having a good time."

At this point, I could see the look that Rachel was giving me. I don't think she had ever seen me put my foot down like that. Not that I was giving her the strongest ultimatum, but listen, this is what I wanted. A lot of my weekends were at home. It's not like I was out and about spending thousands of thousands dollars. I was in the comfort of our home. If she didn't want to be a part of that, fine. But there's no way I was giving in anymore. Over the past three years, I had given in plenty of times to my wife, and this was the time that I decided to be a little selfish for a change

"Fine Rick, I'm out of here. See you later."

And so she left. So I went to the backyard and continued with the party. I found my buddy, Jim, who kept bugging me to go motorcycle riding like we used to back in the good old days. I just hadn't had time for that. Any time I spent away from work and away from the house was at the beach. But it was good to hang out with him again. Good to catch up. He just recently got married and they were expecting their first child. I had to ask him what was it like having sex when the wife clearly didn't want to have sex. His response, "Well, I get what I can and when she doesn't want to do it, I don't get anything." I guess I wasn't alone.

"Jim, I just don't get it. To Rachel, sex almost seems dirty to her. Sometimes I feel like I'm taking advantage of her just to have sex. She's my wife. She should want to have sex. But what can I say; she is just not into it. I understand her drive isn't like mine, but she's accusing me of just marrying her for her body. I told her that I have plenty of options if I wanted…"

"Whoa! Whoa! Whoa! You said what?"

"I was just trying to explain to her that I didn't marry her for sex. That's the point I was trying to get across."

"Yeah but I'm assuming you could've said it in a better way."

"Perhaps, but I'm just tired of walking on egg shells around her and compromising on everything. Everywhere she goes, she spends all kinds of money without considering how I feel. She does this on her own. She sure loves her independence. Look, I'm not saying I want to get rid of her, but something has to change."

At this point, another high school buddy of mine walked up to me.

"Hey Rick, I got this extra ticket to the hockey game tonight, wanna go?"

"Outstanding! Let's go!"

So I called Rachel at her parents. Naturally Rachel asked what time exactly I was planning on getting home. I responded, "Late." Later that night after the hockey game, we went back to my buddy's house to throw some darts. He invited a couple more guys over for a mini-dart tournament.

"Ok just a couple of rounds, but I gotta get home. Rachel is going to kill me."

Before I knew it, it was 5 a.m. and I was still throwing darts and in no condition to drive home. At that point I thought about calling Rachel. I knew I was in for an ass chewing. Wanting to avoid that all together, I decided to wake up the next morning and go to the beach with some of the guys. I could go home in the morning to catch some sleep, but I was sure I was going to get a lecture from Rachel, so I figured I'd save that until later.

I got back the house at about four o'clock and I just knew that Rachel was waiting for me. As soon as I pulled in, my neighbor came out, "Hey Rick, I got tickets the Lakers game, let's go." I don't know if Rachel heard us at that very moment but her timing was impeccable. As soon as I was about to jump in his car, Rachel came out and began to yell as loud as her soft voice could, "Get your ass in the house!"

I then told my neighbor, "I think I better pass, but thanks anyways."

As we walked in the front door, I knew she was ready to lay into me. But all I could think of was what a great weekend I had had. It just might have been worth it.

"Rick, why the hell didn't you come home last night?"

"Honestly, I knew you were going to reprimand me so I just wanted to avoid it as long as possible."

"Unacceptable Rick. You are a married man and you are supposed to be home every night."

"Rachel, I understand what you're saying, but I had too much to drink, and by that point I couldn't drive."

"I just don't understand you. You used to put me first. That hasn't been the case lately."

"Hey, I don't remember the last time you've put me first. You got your job and your parents and the salon and the mall and your credit cards. I feel like I'm probably sixth or seventh on your totem pole of priorities."

"Don't change the subject. This is about you. I want to understand all these parties you seem to need to throw."

"Rachel, I just want to have fun on the weekends. Let's just sit down and have a nice Sunday night dinner just you and me."

Rachel agreed. She cooked a nice dinner, candles, and champagne. We enjoyed ourselves. Naturally, afterwards, I had to take advantage and fulfill my libido. This time she was somewhat giving and was actually excited for a change. It was the first time in a while that we had sex when she hadn't refused at first. A great end to a great week.

I got home the next Friday afternoon to find out the same crowd was setting up at the pool and we were ready for round two. It looked to be another crazy weekend. Luckily I had beat Rachel home. I tried to plead to my buddies to keep it down. My buddy Jim chimed in and said that everyone was already on their way over. Girls too. As he said that, Rachel walked in the door. Clearly she was not having it.

"So how long is this party going to go on?"

"Rachel, I just came home and found this myself."

"Don't you see it as a problem that your friends are setting up their party at our house?"

"They have always known they have free reign to come set up the party and hang out. Nothing has changed."

"Rick, I need you tell everybody to go home. I don't want to party tonight," she said.

"Rachel, it's Friday night. Join us and have a good time. Tomorrow after you get off work, you and I will spend the whole day and whole weekend together doing whatever you want to do. Just have fun tonight with our friends."

"Rick, these are your friends. These are not my friends. My friends wouldn't come over at all hours of the day or night and do what they want at our house."

"I told you I gave them permission. It's fine. Please come join us."

"Nah, I'm going to the mall."

"Typical, just typical. You would rather go shopping than be here with me on a Friday night. If you want to go, then go."

So she left. I tried to forget about this latest argument, but they seemed to be happening more and more. The party ended with this girl that I remember from high school, not by name, just by her look. Boy did she come into her own. I wound up hanging out with her for a while. Her name was Shannon. We played pool and had a couple of drinks. It was so great to talk to girl and not have to worry about an argument that might take place. She asked about my plans the next day. Caught off guard I said, "I don't know. Rachel has to work until around three."

She replied, "Ok great, I'll see you at noon then."

I heard what she had said, but I didn't really comprehend. Was Shannon really going to come over tomorrow while Rachel was at work?

The next morning Rachel had left early for work. I started refinishing the wood around the house. I decided to clean up, do some yard work and hang out. I put on some music inside the house and that helped me clean and get my mind away from things. I thought a lot about music and sports. As I was cleaning, I found that there was pile of mail that was on the kitchen counter. I decided to sift through it because it looked like we left it untouched for a week. One of the envelopes was a greeting card. I started reading it. An old wedding card. While reading, I could hear my name. At first I thought I was hearing things, but then I turned and sure enough through the back door came Shannon.

"Rick, I tried knocking on your door but the music was too loud."

She was beautiful. She was wearing nothing but a tiny bikini top and a pair of cutoff jeans.

"You should get yourself a beer." I said.

I got myself a cold one too and sat down next to her on the couch. I couldn't quite believe what was happening. In front of us on the coffee table was Rachel's Bible. Feeling slightly awkward sitting next to this woman that was turning me on, I got up to go back to the mail to open another envelope. It was a greeting card and the writing looked familiar, just like Rachel's.

The card read, "Rick, I just wanted you to know that I am sorry that my priorities haven't been on par with yours lately and don't quite know what direction we are headed. It seems like we take one step forward and two steps back. I am very happy with you and I still love you very much and I just wanted to let you know through this note that we're going to have a baby. Please call me when you get this. I love you, Rachel."

My knees were weak. I had to read that note four or five times before it sunk in. That two minutes seemed like a day and a half.

Shannon was still sitting there on the couch perplexed.

All I could seem to blurt out was, "I'm going to be a father!"

"Really? Congratulations."

"Yeah I just found out right now. I don't know what to say. I can't believe it."

"So what should we do now?" She said as she batted her eyes.

"I never thought I would say this, but I think we need to say good-bye."

So she left. Once she was gone, I read the card five or six more times just trying to wrap my mind around the fact that I, Rick Martinez, was going to be a father. I got down on my knees, began to pray, and thanked God for what he bestowed on Rachel and me. I couldn't remember the last time I prayed, but it felt like the right thing to do. And after I said Amen, I began talking to myself.

"Shame on you Rick. Shame on you for having a girl in the house."

I called Rachel at work and begged her to come home. She did. We celebrated. We were about to become parents...

13
PARENTHOOD

There are certain moments in your life that stand out, whether they are good or bad. Moments that might change your life. Moments that might change the life of someone you love. Moments that define you and help you grow or help you choose a direction. I can remember the first time I scored a goal and the feeling it gave me inside. I can remember the day my brother moved out and went to college and the cloud it left over my family. I can remember the day Rags died and how it gave me the first true sad moment of my life. I can remember seeing the Louvre in Paris and how much fun I had in Europe. I felt like king of the mountain. However, when Rachel told me I was going to be a father, it didn't really hit me at first.

We went back and forth about it but finally decided on telling our families at Thanksgiving that Rachel was expecting. As we were getting our congratulations hugs and kisses, I felt like I was in a dream with everything moving in slow motion. We celebrated, we prayed, we dreamt about the future, but let's be honest; we didn't quite know what it really meant for us. So between Thanksgiving and Christmas I went about my days as if nothing had changed or as if nothing was going to change. After all, I didn't know any better. I didn't know how to proceed. Even though I was father to Kaylee and Jack, that situation was purely biological as I was not a part of their lives and was not there for Tara during the pregnancy. Work was still work. We still went to Lake Cachuma. We still had our everyday issues. Truly it seemed like nothing different. Then Christmas night came.

We had spent Christmas Eve with the Parkers up in Lynwood. They had really settled in to a nice house up there and were thoroughly enjoying partial retirement. As we left Christmas morning to head back down to Los Angeles, Wally nudged me ever so slightly and said half-jokingly, "Rick, I know you can see yourself with a place here in the mountains where the air is so clean and everything is so peaceful." He was half right. I did love the mountains but would miss my family so much. Later that night at my parents' house, we exchanged gifts with the rest of the family. My brother, Gil, was calling out names and passing out presents. That long process was nothing new to me or the family. But then he said something that I was just not ready for.

"To Baby, from Nanny and Poppy."

At first, I didn't know what he meant. And then Rachel gave her girly sigh, "Awwwww! Look Rick, it's for the baby!" You see, instead of grandma and grandpa, my parents always wanted to be known as Nana and Tata, tradition in my family. However, Beth's son, the first born grandchild, kept saying Nanny and Poppy, so the names stuck.

They passed me the present, which if anyone knows the shape of a present, it being rectangle meant clothes. I tore through the paper and opened the box to see tiny, yellow pajama sleepers. Everyone in the room just melted. More sighs, "Awwwwwwww!" I started to laugh. And for some reason, it just felt natural to cradle the pajamas as if there was a baby inside them. I buried my face in the top, pretending to kiss the pajamas over and over. It was right then and there that I truly felt like a father-to-be. Within the next year, someone was going to depend on me for their every need. I couldn't wait.

There was this feeling inside of me that was so unsure about what was about to happen. We had waited nearly four years from the time we got married. I thought this was very important because, let's be honest, we were just kids on our wedding day and in some ways we still were. Were we grown up enough to be not only parents, but good, responsible parents? Plus all the fighting, the back-and-forth that Rachel and I went through. Was this baby going to just be a quick fix or had we grown together to the point where we could put our differences aside and be the great parents that this baby deserved?

Then there was also the worry that I was one of those people that just couldn't sit still and I just had so much energy whether with work or surfing or partying and drinking. I guess I was still unsure if I could truly settle down, not just with one woman, but to stay at home on a Friday night to feed the baby. To get up in the middle of the night to feed the baby. The nurturing, changing diapers, putting on their clothes. Was I truly going to have the energy to do all this for the baby? So I decided to use up all this energy and do something I probably would never have done before: I went shopping for the baby and wanted to surprise Rachel at the same time. The surprise came, however, later that night at home.

I was pretty proud of myself. I went shopping for the baby, got all the bottles, got tons of diapers, got the crib and put it together. I was basically putting together the nursery for the baby. Coloring it in mostly yellow because we decided we weren't going to find out if the baby was a boy or a girl. I got all the little things as well: the mobile over the crib and the little toys. I wanted to surprise Rachel and do this not only for the baby, but for her. Her idea of buying for the baby was different than of mine.

You see, at the same time I was building the crib and arranging the nursery just right, she was elsewhere buying baby clothes of course. Not just your typical pajamas, tops, pants, socks, etc. She was buying the best of everything, spending hundreds and hundreds of dollars, not to anyone's surprise or mine, naturally. Part of me wanted to tell her to take it all back. We just didn't need to spend all this money on clothes. We could go bargain shopping, even if it meant going to the secondhand stores, Salvation Army. Rachel was just so excited. She was getting bigger too and she was worried about my desire for her with her changing body. So I decided to be supportive and let her have her way this time, even though it did cost a pretty penny. Even in her third trimester, Rachel was still Rachel to her core.

Luckily for me, Rachel was not hormonal. And any nagging of hers was always forgotten when I got to feel the baby kicking. Even though we were going to wait to find out, the kicking told me it was going to be a girl. Speaking of girls, my mom and sister did throw Rachel an incredible baby shower. Not that I had firsthand knowledge, but Elfrieda did go on and on about the job they did and everything they did for Rachel. Elfrieda and Lindy were truly grateful. I was happy about that, since I could tell that Beth still hadn't warmed up completely to Rachel. But mom made sure, now more than ever with a baby on the way, Beth would not make any waves with Rachel and I.

The due date was rapidly approaching, late July to be specific. We still had yet to decide on girl's names or boy's names. So can you imagine our shock when Rachel began having contractions and went into early labor. We were a little surprised. So were my parents who were planning on a camping vacation but didn't want to leave town without seeing another grandchild born. I was going to be a father soon and they seemed as excited as I was. They were going to be in that waiting room day or night. I got Rachel to the hospital and waiting for us were Wally and Elfrieda. I was grateful for them, especially because we were having a party at our house and they had everything Rachel would need. As we had left for the hospital, our guests hung around and started to clean up the house for us. That was a big help. After all, we would be bringing home a baby soon.

Rachel agonized through more than 24 hours of labor. The doctors figured it was taking too much of a toll on her and the baby. The best option was to induce. Not too long after, I saw the birth of my first child. IT'S A GIRL! I shouted at just past one o'clock in the morning on July 21, 1985. After a few minutes, I decided and Rachel agreed on the name, Lindsey Martinez. She was perfect. We spent the rest of the night just settling in, gazing in to each others' eyes as well as the eyes of our new miracle. We began to cry. It seemed like yesterday that I was just a kid relying on mom and dad to feed me, clothe me and look after my every need. Time had flown by and now I was a father. It was surreal.

Rachel begged me to go home and get some sleep. Elfreida said that she would stay with the new mother through the night. I told them I would be back later that morning to relieve Elfrieda from looking after Rachel. When I walked through my front door, everyone was still there partying, but they went silent right before I yelled again, IT'S A GIRL! A big celebration followed. Cigars, champagne and beer for everyone. Also surreal. In the past, we celebrated wins on the soccer field. We celebrated holidays. We celebrated music. We found many reasons to celebrate. This time, we celebrated Rick Martinez's newborn daughter. As we were about to really get into the partying, a buddy of mine came over to say good-bye. I begged him to stay and enjoy the fun. Then he floored me. "Hey Rick, you're a father now. Get some sleep." So everyone left and I did. He was right. It was time for me to be more responsible. There was a little girl who needed me. I may not have always put Rachel first, but Lindsey was going to be put first, last and everywhere in between.

Mom and dad stayed around for the day we brought Lindsey home from the hospital. Nanny and Poppy had another grandchild, number six for them. As I was holding Lindsey, mom mentioned how ironic it was that I was holding her in pretty much the exact same spot of the house she used to hold me when I was a baby. Another surreal moment. As they left that night, dad hugged me and congratulated me. Then he reminded me, "We start at six tomorrow morning. Don't be late."

Getting home from work that day was different. My daughter was waiting for me, but that specific day was different for another reason. As I was about to open the door, Elfrieda busted through it with tears.

"Rick! Rick! She's hemorrhaging. We have to do something."

"Who? Lindsay?"

"No, Rachel!"

"Ok Elfrieda, calm down. Put Lindsey in her car seat and I'll get Rachel."

She looked exhausted. We rushed to the hospital and immediately got her checked in at the ER. We just left this hospital a few days ago, and now we were back. After a few hours, the doctor said Rachel was ok and that she just needed rest but would have to stay there a few days for monitoring. So once again, Elfrieda stayed with Rachel and I went home. But this time, I took Lindsey with me. And while I was concerned about Rachel and her well being, the next few days would be some of the happiest of my life. I got to spend every waking moment with Lindsey and I couldn't get enough of it.

Forgetting that she already had a case of colic. Forgetting that she had these patches of hair all over her scalp. Forgetting that she was going through diapers at a record pace. I absolutely loved having this quality time, just Lindsey and me. I told her stories. I sang to her with my guitar. This took me some time because I hadn't picked my old dove up for months. But mostly I just watched her. I watched her breathe. I watched her sleep. I even watched her cry a little. This was all so new and exciting for me. I wanted every day to be like this. Lindsey was a blessing to Rachel and I. Parenthood made me feel like king of the mountain again.

14
TRAGEDIES

Being a full time father for the first time was the best, but also a little nerve racking. You talk about having to watch someone every single minute, every single second of every day. It was a second full-time job. Naturally I was still working full-time as well. But 4 a.m. feedings with Lindsay resulted in me arriving early at the job site, something even dad was even happy to see. Don't get me wrong, we still had parties on the weekends, but not as crazy as before. Less beer, more formula and more baby proofing. Our Lindsey, with her nasally voice and patches of hair, seemed to have so many quirky little things about her. She had my eyes and her mother's nose and smile. After a couple months, Rachel went back to work and she was actually looking forward to it. She worked her way into a better position at the hospital where Lindsey was born.

With both of us at work and Lindsay still a baby, we needed to hire a babysitter. We hired a high school girl that lived down the street whose job was to fill in when both Rachel and I were working and when neither my parents nor the Parkers couldn't watch the baby. It turned out that Rachel would call the sitter many, many times to assist her or be the mother while Rachel would relax. This went on for a few weeks without me knowing. Finally, the sitter spoke up. I wasn't surprised. She simply stated that Rachel was not best of mothers. She was not good at keeping a keen eye on Lindsay. It was hard to hear at first, but we were new parents. I wanted to talk to Rachel about it, but I had no idea how to approach her. I was a novice at this myself. So I just told the sitter to please let me know if this gets any worse and to please be on top of things.

It only took a year for Rachel to fall back into her spending habits. The Camaro was nowhere close to being paid off, but she decided she had enough of that and traded it in for a brand new Mercedes. Six months after that, she became frightened that someone would hit the car so she bought a Subaru. Neither decision did she talk with me. She still didn't get it. Not only did our budget need to change because of our little girl, but now she wasn't considering a car that might be more conducive for a child. Would this ever change? I guess I was a little at fault. I still couldn't say no to Rachel, even after six years of marriage.

The night of Lindsay's second birthday, I sang her to sleep with Alabama's "Never be One." She was just two and I was already becoming nostalgic about having a baby in the house. So I subconsciously overlooked Rachel's lack of parental expertise and, oops, another pregnancy. This was not necessarily planned but I was ecstatic just the same when I found that note a few weeks later from Rachel that we were expecting baby number two. Right away we were picking out names. We decided not to find out if it was a boy or girl but deep down I was hoping for a boy. Of course, I was hoping the baby was just healthy. Six months went by and all was well until that day I got home from work and Rachel was waiting at the door.

"Something is wrong Rick. I can just feel the baby is not right."

"How can you be so sure? Are you alright?"

"I just have this feeling inside and it's not good."

"Ok Rachel, let's get you to the hospital."

I could tell Rachel was upset and worried but deep down I knew that everything would be fine. Rachel would stay overnight, perhaps a few nights, but in the end, all would be fine. Maybe Rachel was overdoing it. Maybe she was working too many hours. Maybe she was on her feet too much. Once released from the hospital, I would make sure to keep her bedridden if need be. The doctor ran a few tests and we waited. And waited. And waited some more. Finally, after a few hours, the doctor came back in the room.

"So Doc, how is the baby? How is Rachel?

"Oh, the baby is dead."

Just like that. We were stunned. Not only had we just lost our baby, but the way he gave us the bad news was enough to send shivers down my spine and make my blood boil. No concern from the doctor. No emotion. Just a cold, life altering statement. It took every bit of me not to punch the doctor's lights out. How dare he come at us the way he did? Then after a few moments, my madness turned to deep sorrow and dismay. I tried not to cry, to be strong for Rachel. Looking at her, she clearly had no emotion. She had a blank look on her face. I hugged her and kissed her on her forehead. I started to tear up but was still able to check my emotions. Rachel's face was still blank. I was going through a bunch of firsts in my life and none of them were good. Other than my dog, Rags, I had never lost anything or anyone and never to this magnitude. A few more minutes of silence went by and I finally mustered up a few words to the doctor.

"So what happens next?"

"Well, we will have to induce labor and Rachel will have to give birth to the fetus. Rachel, this is the only way."

I waited for Rachel to answer, but still nothing from her.

"Ok Doc, if that's what you have to do, then let's do it." I said.

By the end of the night, Rachel had given birth to our dead baby. I will never forget what that looked like. Finally, after an hour of plain nothing, Rachel burst into tears and asked if we could go home. As we lay on our bed, I tried to comfort my wife. In my mind, we lost the baby simply because it was meant to be. I looked at it as if something would have been wrong long-term with the baby. Rachel wasn't ready to buy into it. She wasn't ready for anything. Weeks went by before she seemed back to normal. She would break down at any instant. Somehow, she found her answers at church. Her sister Lindy had convinced her to try religion and possibly find comfort that way. I was all for it. I was all for anything that helped my wife get clarity and get some sort of closure. Life is hard and this was quite a lesson we were learning. Again, another way I was trying to look at it.

Finally, Rachel expressed that she wanted to get away from things. Vacation, yeah. Let's go to Mammoth. Let's go to Vegas. Let's get away. Rachel's definition wasn't exactly that. She wanted to sell the house, get rid of anything that reminded her of current everyday life. She found a house not too far from her old neighborhood, near where her, Wally and Elfrieda used to live. It was a nice house and we sold the Penfield house right away. Even made a nice profit from it. The only two negatives were that I had to say goodbye to my childhood home, and I had to say goodbye to the pool. The new place, in Agoura Hills, was a beautiful two story house with a Jacuzzi and seemed like a great neighborhood to raise a family. Plus, it wasn't the worst thing in the world to move twenty minutes farther away from Mom and Dad and the rest of the family. They could be a bit overwhelming at times.

We settled in just after Christmas and Rachel was back to being Rachel. Shopping of course and going to the salon. She even bought herself a mink that cost more than a pretty penny. This time, I didn't mind. Not only was she stunning when wearing a nice dress, but I was just happy she was happy. It took us weeks to take down all the Christmas decorations and cards. All things considered, it had been a good holiday season. We even reread the cards a few times. We were extremely touched by Chad and Lindy's card. They loved Lindsay like their own. They had decided not to have a child because of Chad being albino and not wanting a child of theirs to be teased and picked on as much as he was growing up. Lindy could be difficult, to put it mildly, and Chad, not Wally or Elfreida was the one person who could keep her in check. Spending time with the Parker family was tolerable, but even more so when Chad was around. He wore a suit and tie every day, but a down to earth, great guy.

Rachel was on her way home from work on Valentine's Day and with Lindsay over at Mom and Dad's, I was preparing the typical romantic candlelight dinner. I was on the phone with mom all day trying to get the perfect advice for the perfect gourmet meal. So when the phone rang again, I was ready to tell mom that I think I had it all taken care of. But a different voice was on the line.

"Rick, it's Lindy, is Rachel there?"

"No sweetie, she hasn't gotten home from work yet. What's wrong?"

"Chad was in a head on collision and died on impact."

Lindy was crying almost out of control. I didn't really know what to say except, "Oh Lindy, I'm so sorry. What can I do?"

"I don't know Rick; I am just so lost. Can you have Rachel call me?"

"Absolutely. I'll call the airlines and see what flights we can make. We'll be there as soon as we can."

I don't know why but when I hung up the phone, all I could think about was how Rachel would feel. It had been a few months since we lost the baby and she seemed to have moved on from it. When she got home, I broke the news to her as gently as possible. I assured her that I was here for her and her family. Wally called just after that and let us know that he booked tickets for Rachel, Lindsay and I for the red eye

86

that night. We would arrive in Missouri by morning. Chad's service was the following day. At the funeral parlor, we all gathered around and prayed before and after. It was a very small service with a beautiful choir and an open coffin. As I said goodbye to him I couldn't help but think he looked like he was taking a nap. Walking back to my seat, I saw out of the corner of my eye Rachel hugging and talking with a woman I had never met before. Well, until now.

"Rick, I want you to meet my mother, Dottie. Mom, this is my husband Rick. Rick, go get Lindsay. I want her to meet her grandmother."

This was surreal. It took me a moment to grasp what was going on. Luckily, I had time while getting Lindsay to get my bearings. I had known Rachel for about seven years and was finally meeting her biological mother. I brought Lindsay over and before I could finish saying how nice it was to meet her, she cut me off.

"Give me my granddaughter."

Not quite the reception I was expecting, but ok, I can roll with that. I could see the huge smile on Dottie's face. The same smile that Rachel showed the night I met her. Dottie's was beaming with pride, holding the grandchild she never knew. Perhaps even trying to buy back time that she lost with her kids. It had been a few years since Lindy and Chad had migrated to Joplin, Missouri. Mainly to get to know her estranged mother whom had left her so many years ago. She took Lindsay over to the choir and held Lindsay up in her arms, as if to show her off. I was just about to check on Rachel and Lindy to see how they were when the Brother came over.

"Hi Brother, I'm Rick Martinez. It was a lovely service.

"Thank you for attending, Rick. I am Brother Scarborough. How do you do?"

Now my mind was running all over the place and if I wasn't sure, the look on Rachel's face confirmed what I already knew. This was the man rumored to take Dottie away. I had already heard whispers that day from Elfrieda and even some of the choir members that this man had Dottie and her trailer with him at his ranch. After a few pleasantries, I could tell that this Brother was not a straight shooter. I was surveying the room and soaking in everything like a sponge. Elfreida was not happy at all being upstaged by Dottie, the new and pretend grandmother. Wally and Adam were done with this all and were ready to head back to the hotel for a drink at the bar. What happened in the next few minutes spoke volumes. I could see that Dottie big smile turned to disgust. She bee lined her way over to me and demanded, "Your daughter needs to be changed."

Brother Scarborough had finally left but not before giving me a dirty look. To put it politely, he was a questionable man. I was actually relieved when he left. After I changed Lindsay, I had Elfrieda take her back to the hotel with Wally and Adam. I stayed and sat back, watching Rachel and Lindy catch up with Dottie. It was an education. Here was this woman who gave up her kids for nothing, and here they were hanging on her every word. They talked for an hour, exchanged photos of Lindsay and then a very big and tight embrace. I had never seen Rachel hug Wally or Elfreida that way. Hell, I had never seen Rachel hug Lindsay that way. I was stunned. I ran to the phone to call and thank mom and dad for being amazing parents.

We went back to the hotel that night for some dinner. I was exhausted. Everybody was exhausted. Everyone except Rachel. With Lindsay sound asleep in Wally and Elfreida's room, Rachel decided that she wanted to go out. Perhaps this was the first time she had to talk me into going out. We didn't say much that night but I could still tell how alive Rachel was. I was dying to know how her conversation went with her biological mother, but I didn't dare ask. I figured if she wanted to talk about it, she would bring it up. It was a neat little town. Just a couple of main roads, some restaurants and honky-tonk bars, no mountains, only hills. This was the Bible belt and I was enjoying it. Then Rachel opened up a bit.

"I love it here Rick. Couldn't you see yourself living here?"

"Uh, no!"

"Why not Rick? Lindy said that the cost of living is nothing compared to southern California. The people are so nice here."

"Rachel, we just bought a nice, big house in a great neighborhood. I can't wait to get home."

"But Rick, Lindy loves the church. I told Brother Scarborough how great you were with music. He wants you to play guitar in the choir. Give it some thought."

"Rachel, I love you, but we're not moving here. I'm tired. Let's go back to the hotel and get some sleep."

The next morning Rachel was up and gone. I went to Wally and Elfreida's room to get Lindsay, change her diaper and feed her. Wally mentioned that Lindy and Rachel went to church and would be back in an hour. When they rolled up in the rental car, Rachel got out of the passenger's side and professed her love for God, this town and that we had to move here. Lindy followed with a sermon of her own. I had to stop this.

"Rachel, how about this? If we can sell the house in Agoura Hills, we can look for some property up north a bit in Oakhurst, perhaps not too far from your parents and move there. Let's do that."

Rachel stood still for a moment and then agreed. After my umpteenth compromise, this southern California guy was leaving the big city and heading to central California in the hick town mountains. Was I really ready for this?

15
CONFLICT

We had gotten back to southern California and somehow managed to put Missouri in the rear view mirror. I knew what I had committed to do. I knew what it meant to Rachel. Deep down, though, I didn't think she would keep me to that promise. So I decided not to bring it up and pretend like it never happened, which was very easy for me. Not even counting the time spent at home with Lindsay, my little toddler, let alone work was crazy. I didn't know I could work so many hours in a day and in a week. My surfboards and my fishing poles collected dust in the garage. No weekend trips or getaways were possible to plan. I was lucky to keep my head above water. Not that I minded the money. Lord knows it was good money.

Dad was giving me more responsibility which led to financial motivation. And even though my brother joined the company as president in waiting, I felt like I was getting the complete respect from Dad and Gil that I rightfully deserved. I never truly loved getting up before the crack of dawn to go to work but now at least it seemed easier for me. They even gave me the go ahead and the down payment to buy a company truck. At first I was excited but decided to tell Dad that he should get one, sort of like a retirement gift.

He had been contemplating retiring for some time now but no one ever believed him. He seemed pretty serious about it but there were two things that said he wouldn't do it. One, he never liked to leave things in the hands of others. Even when I was a kid and our family was going away for the weekend, Dad was hard to get along with that day because he constantly worried about what he was leaving, even if it was just for a day. Most of the time he was leaving things with his brother, my uncle, but that didn't stop him from worrying. One time we got to Lake Cachuma and right after we set up camp and Mom started cooking dinner, Dad abruptly got out of his chair and yelled, "Pack everything up, we're leaving." And we did. Us kids didn't whine or complain. We knew that would make things worse. Plus, we saw how upset Mom was. Actually, let me rephrase, she was mad. Never saw her mad before. So that was one reason I never thought he would retire. He loved to work. The second reason I didn't think he would retire was because I didn't think he would find anything to keep him entertained. He had been working since he was fourteen years old. It was all he knew and no coaxing by me or Gil or Mom could get him to retire. He had to do it on his own. When it was time for me to get my company truck, I wish he had retired. That's when things went bad.

First, I saw that my brother Gil was getting a brand new BMW. I didn't love the idea that he was getting that and I was getting a truck but I never said anything. I figured I would need a truck on the jobsites. Plus, how am I going to argue when I was given $1500 for the down payment. However, this money was given with a condition. I had to run any possible decision to purchase by my dad and Gil. I had found a great 4-wheel drive and worked the salesman down to a pretty good price. As he began getting the papers together, I called my dad. His words, "Nah, what the hell do you want a 4-wheel drive for? You're going to wreck it." Even though I was thirty years old and completely able to sign the papers myself, he still felt I didn't know any better. Finally, he came to some sort of agreement. "Ask your brother. If he says yes, then you can get it."

Naturally I didn't quite get why I had to ask my brother if I could get a certain car, but to keep the peace, I dialed the phone. Line busy. I tried a handful of times but to no avail. Frustrated with that and with the whole situation, I made an executive decision. I was getting this truck and there was nothing my Dad or Gil could say to stop me. You see, it was a beautiful truck, just like the one I had in high school. And although I did wreck that one on a fun night in the hills, that was a long time ago. I was a man now.

I rolled into my Mom and Dad's house so excited to show Dad and Gil the new truck. Mom had turned one of the rooms in their house into an office. She was still helping with the books even though Dad was half way to retirement. They came outside to my honking the horn.

"Rick, what in the hell are you doing?!"

"Dad, the truck is perfect and it was great deal."

"I said I didn't want that 4-wheel drive on the jobsites. Did you ask Gil? Did you ask me?

"Dad, I'm sorry. I tried calling from the dealership but the line was busy. I couldn't get through."

After a few minutes, Gil chimed in.

"Dad, don't worry about it. I'm sure it will be fine. Besides, if it's going to be Rick's, he should get something he likes. I gotta go but we'll talk more tonight."

The family was to have dinner at the White Horse Inn to celebrate. Gil had signed papers on a huge deal for the company. This contract was by far the biggest and best for the family business. We all left the kids at home with baby sitters and got all dressed up for the celebration. The food was as good as always. The wine and liquor flowed like nothing you've ever seen before. The family had always stayed close. It seemed like every weekend we were over at Mom and Dad's with Gil's family, Beth's family and my own. It actually became a little smothering at times but I knew my Mom wanted it that way. Who am I kidding? They both wanted it that way. And it was even more so since Lindsey was born. Dad would call and would immediately ask, "You coming over? You gonna bring the baby?" Saying we had plans or that we just wanted to stay home and relax for a day was simply out of the question.

But tonight at the restaurant, we were all having a good time. When dessert was being served, Dad stood and clinked his glass for a toast, something he almost never did.

"I want to thank everyone for being here tonight. This is a great night for the family and for the business. I am very proud of where the company is and the road we have taken to get to this point. A lot of work, a lot of man hours and a lot of sacrifice."

I could see Mom and Beth's eyes well up with tears. We all knew he was officially retiring. What a great moment for him. He continued.

"When we were putting Gil through college, the sacrifices became a little tougher. But I always knew that those tough sacrifices would pay off. I knew that Gil was going to be the man he is today. He works hard. He makes great choices, and seeing how he has steered the company into bigger and better things, I couldn't be prouder of a man, of my son. Gil, I love you and thank you for getting the contract. It's your company now."

I knew what that meant and I was truly happy. Everyone was happy for Gil. He did deserve it. But then Dad stood up again. I guess he had one more thing to say.

"And then there is Rick..."

And he just dropped his head and shook it in jest. People sort of laughed uncomfortably. Yes, he was trying to make a joke, but I didn't appreciate it at all. I was floored actually. Knocked out like a prize fighter lying on the canvas. I truly thought I had come a long way with work and building a family of my own. And in my father's eyes, I was the same old Rick. I knew something had to change. As Rachel and I drove home that night, I told her it was time to move to Oakhurst. I was done with the whole scene. The family, the business, the whole thing. Screw it. I was done with it all and wanted to get away. It felt like I was living at home all over again. Not able to do anything without my parents say so, without Dad's approval. The only way to get out, in my mind, was to get far away.

We didn't tell the family when we officially put the house up for sale but when the herds of people starting swarming the open houses, we figured it was just a matter of time. At first, I thought it was better to do this in person. When I called my parents to tell them we had something to say, mom's words, "Oh no, what's wrong?" I reassured her that nothing was wrong and that we were all just fine. I ended up inviting them out to brunch, a public place where no one could lose their head. We ordered and then Dad cut right to the chase.

"Ok, what seems to be the problem?"

"No problem, Dad. Rachel and I have decided to move to Oakhurst."

"Oh Mijo, that's too far!" Mom cried out with her high pitched voice. Rachel and I couldn't help but laugh even though she was sad. Dad put his head down and muttered,

"You sure this is what you want to do?"

"Yeah Dad, it's time for us to be on our own. We feel a little cramped here with the family and its better for us to get away and start a new life elsewhere."

I could tell they weren't too happy but they actually took it fairly well, which made things very easy for us. Naturally, Wally and Elfreida were ecstatic. They were going to see their granddaughter all the time.

When visiting them to start looking for a place to live, I knew exactly what I wanted. Oakhurst was a small town, population 15,000. This was perfect in my mind. A place where everyone waves hello as you drive by but with the size of the land, no one looking over your shoulder or fence. Definitely big enough where Rachel and I could build our dream home. Build it the way we wanted. We found the perfect piece of property right away. Three acres, plenty of room to run around, and overlooking part of the community. Right away, we were talking about marble counter tops, wood burning stoves and a fence to keep Lindsay in and the critters out. We even decided we would buy a basset hound once we moved in our new place.

Instead of going surfing, I knew that I would go fishing as often as possible. After all, the property was less than five miles from a lake. I was envisioning the largemouth bass I could mount over that wood burning stove. Once the house in Agoura was sold, we could buy the land and start building. Luckily for us, the house sold in less than three months. And even luckier for us, we made a nice profit, especially only being in this house for three years.

We were like busy beavers packing things up. The excitement was overflowing within us. Before we left for the mountains, we decided to have one more romantic weekend at the beach. I had one more morning of surfing at Zuma. Who knew when I would get the chance to do that again? Then Rachel and I went out for a very intimate, very loving evening. Dining by candlelight and dancing while the sun was setting. I couldn't help myself. I took Rachel down to the shore. I commandeered a couple of blankets nearby and was convinced that we were going to conceive a child. With this new change and new beginning in a new town, we were definitely ready to expand our family.

The next morning, driving in the U-Haul out of the valley and up Interstate 5, Rachel leaned over, "You know, I could be pregnant the next time I take the test."

"I know you are."

What a great feeling it was. Despite leaving my home town, the big city, the beach, the nightlife and my family, I was ready to break away. I was ready to rejuvenate myself and start anew. Oakhurst, here comes the Martinez family.

16
OAKHURST

1989 was the best time in my adult life. Lindsay, now almost four years old, was very happy in her new pre-school and very happy with the idea of being a big sister. She seemed to be adjusting well to her new home and spending a lot of time with Rachel's parents. Rachel was just into her second trimester of pregnancy and had virtually no morning sickness. All signs were just what the doctor ordered and thoughts of a repeat miscarriage didn't seem to be in the cards. We both decided that it was better she not work during pregnancy, just to be on the safe side. Our house was finished and although there was little stuff to do around the yard, it was our dream home. Thanks to Wally and because of some other people we had gotten to know in past visits, I was able to pick up some jobs here and there, mostly doing tile work and other projects in houses. Because our southern California house sold for the right price, it gave me the flexibility to set my own schedule. I could work a day or two a week and enjoy what the town and the surrounding areas had to offer. And although it was not Los Angeles, in a lot of ways it was a good thing. Something I never thought would be true.

My typical day would start by waking up between 7:00-8:00 a.m. I might go out back and have a cigarette. I might sit out front and read the paper. If it were too cold in the morning, which meant snow on the ground, I'd watch some TV by our wood burning stove. Around the time I put another log on the fire, Lindsay would wake up and waddle over to me with her bed head and pink barrette to one side. She would take my place on the floor and I would make breakfast. Her favorite cartoons were Minnie Mouse, Tom & Jerry, and Bugs Bunny.

I would get a kick out of her repeating the lines in her cute four-year old vocabulary and nasally voice.

After breakfast, we would go and wake up Rachel, who would sleep all day if we let her. A few minutes of cuddle time and then Rachel would start to get in the shower and get ready. I got Lindsay dressed and ready to take to pre-school. By the time I got back home, Rachel was ready. We'd throw together some stuff for a picnic and be on the road. It was only forty-five minutes to the heart of the Yosemite Valley and the drive there was half the fun. George Strait or Alabama would be in the cassette player and I would be singing to Rachel and our baby in her tummy. Once in Yosemite, we'd stop and walk a little, discovering some beautiful scenery. Then we'd drive a little further, stop and set up a blanket for our lunch in a small meadow just near a creek, not too far from some deer. Rachel and I would chit chat, laugh, reminisce about the days we met and started dating. It was very romantic and very quiet, as if we had the whole valley to ourselves.

Around 1 p.m. we'd pack up and head back. Naturally, Rachel had to stop at some little shop and get some knick-knack for the house or for herself. We'd swing by to pick up Lindsay from school, then stop off at Wally and Elfreida's for a little while just to visit. By the late afternoon/early evening, we would stop off for dinner. For a small town, Oakhurst did have a variety of restaurants. The town had everything from Danny's Pizza to The Grill to our favorite, The Mountain House. I'd get the filet mignon or T-bone steak. Rachel would order chicken or salmon. Lindsay always seemed to enjoy spaghetti. Not the taste of it, but the playing with it and getting it all over her face. Dessert was always an option, probably some chocolate mousse or tiramisu. We loved tiramisu. It seemed like an aphrodisiac for us. Which lead us to putting Lindsay to bed, not before singing to her and playing my guitar until she fell asleep. Then Rachel and I headed to our bedroom for our intimate finish to the evening. That was our typical day in our new life.

You see, while growing up and living in southern California, I was fortunate to see lots of the country, even Canada and parts of Europe. But I always considered southern California my whole world. Now, my world was growing. And Oakhurst, especially after living in a big city, definitely seemed like another world. And I was falling in love with it. There were days I would head to the lake and catch my limit of bass, scale them and fry them for a nice dinner. I never saw myself as a golfer, well except when I was laughing my ass off watching Rodney Dangerfield in Caddyshack. However, I bought a set of used clubs and began to play a couple of times a week at the course, again just a couple miles away. By this time, I had made a few friends, either from buying supplies for my side jobs or just because everyone in Oakhurst was so friendly and warm. At first they were quiet when hearing I was from the big city of Los Angeles, but after the ice was broken, they were more than willing to share a case of beer at the lake, the driving range or at Danny's Pizza.

Rachel took a little longer to make friends in Oakhurst but she was never lonely. She had her best friends, Visa and MasterCard, to entertain her like always. Buying for the nursery took her all day. After all, not knowing if she was buying for a boy or a girl, she bought for both. Our credit card statement got longer and longer. Then, of course, she took it upon herself to furnish the new house with the finest Oakhurst could offer. Well at least the finest antiques. I guess she found shopping easy wherever she went and wherever she lived.

As spring turned into summer, Rachel got bigger and bigger. The obstetrician Elfrieda had recommended was very warm and helpful to Rachel. Each doctor's visit seemed to be one thumbs up after another. We were getting excited that the baby was almost here. One thing Oakhurst had in common with southern California was the tremendous heat. Late June and early July had a long streak of triple-digit temperatures. This was particularly irritating to Rachel on nights when she couldn't sleep.

The Fourth of July was a big celebration in Oakhurst. Everyone in town as well as many out of towners would go to the lake and spend all day there. Some friends invited Rachel, Lindsay and I on their boat for a day of fun on the water. This was going to be perfect. I could get some water skiing in, maybe some fishing too, and still have my two favorite girls by my side when the fireworks started at sunset. That's not exactly how that day went in Oakhurst. If you weren't on or at the lake by 9 a.m. on the Fourth of July, you were in trouble. That place was a zoo. We did get on the lake with our friends, but so did hundreds of other boats. No water skiing or fishing that day. Only the jet skis were small enough to move around the lake. Jet Skiers and boaters didn't seem to get along on the lake. They each thought the lake belonged to them. There were so many boats on the lake by the time the fireworks started, you could literally walk from one boat to the next and make it from one shore to the other. It wound up being pretty fun but something Rachel and I vowed to never do again on the Fourth.

We did spend many other days on the water that first summer. Rachel would claim to have a headache almost every day and the only things that seemed to cure it were shopping or the lake. You can guess what I always voted for. Plus, I always felt it was important for Lindsay to grow up around bodies of water. I had both the ocean and lakes growing up. She at least had the lake and learned to love the water and how to swim almost right away. Just watching Lindsay's every move, I still marveled at how lucky we were that she was happy and healthy. Deep down I was praying that the baby coming was going to also be healthy.

August 19th happened to be the hottest day of that summer and wouldn't you know that was the day that Rachel went into labor. She did have a wonderful pregnancy, no morning sickness and no false alarms, so when she went into labor that morning, we knew the baby would soon be here. Wally and Elfrieda met us at the hospital. Once we got there, I had Elfrieda help Rachel in the room while I took a minute to get on the pay phone and call my parents. They were on their way. Hopefully Rachel and the baby would cooperate for 4 hours so they could be there for yet another grandchild's birth.

Everyone says that their baby is perfect at birth but you know that can't be true of every baby. However, for our newborn girl, Aubrey, she truly was. Rachel had no trouble at all with the delivery and when the doctor laid Aubrey in blankets and put her in Rachel's arms, I swear she was perfect. It was like she came out already cleaned and washed off. She almost had this angelic appeal to her. Rachel was also lying in bed as if it was just another day. She was chatting with Lindsay and the doctor. You would never know that she just went through hours of labor. Both pairs of grandparents were in the waiting room when I ran out to yell, "It's a girl! We got another girl! She looks perfect and Rachel did great. We can't wait for you to see her."

We brought Aubrey home from the hospital a couple of days later and she still looked perfect. She also had the most perfectly round shaped head I had ever seen. She almost looked like a porcelain doll. I loved the feeling of being a father again. We had been in Oakhurst for about six months and I felt like the luckiest man in the world.

17
ASPIRATIONS

As the leaves began to turn golden brown, awaiting their wistful journey to the ground, I was granted one more glorious summer-like day in late September to enjoy the nearby lake before Oakhurst's cruel autumn chill would rule the waters inhospitable to man until the following spring. Hopping over the small wakes while windsurfing, I reflected back on my nearly 30 years of life. I couldn't imagine that anybody had more fun than me. As much as I thoroughly enjoyed making love to those multitudes of beautiful women, and reflecting on those masterpieces, life was great being a father to Lindsay and Aubrey. And now I was living in my idea of paradise. But for some reason, Rachel wasn't included in my perfect vision. Sure, she still turned me on, and I definitely loved her, but there were times where I just couldn't stand being around her.

Her parents definitely didn't help. Elfrieda was a bossy know-it-all with what seemed like an obscene affection for stray cats. There were always at least ten felines occupying the in-laws' premises, leaving the house reeking of cat spray and soiled kitty litter. And Wally seemed to be losing his mind ever since he retired. Living with Elfreida, not to mention his three kids, he wasn't all that sane to begin with, anyway.

I jumped one last wave wake with a spinning flourish to reach the shore. And then, I was alone. I remembered my days of water skiing as an adolescent and tried to decipher if wind surfing now, as opposed to water skiing, had something to do with me growing up and being an adult. I did enjoy and embrace the momentary solitude Rachel had granted me, a reward for providing her with a full night's sleep for the first time since we came home with Aubrey. I sat down on the towel

I had spread out by the side of the lake and took in the magnificent wilderness before me. It was then that I found myself wishing my old buddies from L.A. could be with me to see this amazing view. If there was ever a way to transport my friends from 1980 to present day, this portrait would be complete. Sure, the local guys in Oakhurst were cool enough, but they couldn't relate to the varied environments that I had grown accustomed to in the big city. It had been years since they saw a woman who didn't sport a tattoo, drive a truck, or chug beer. My co-workers' tastes in movies never veered from on screen bullets, blood and boobs. Their idea of fine dining was a restaurant that didn't have sawdust on the floor. And they never laid eyes on a lady as fine as Shelley.

Damn! There she was again. Shelley. Entering my most private thoughts and memories. What was Shelly doing now? Did she ever get married? Have kids? Is she in charge of her family's business? With that last question, I started to fume about how my father denied me that right. I realized then that I had the ability to start a business of my own and without needing anybody else's help. Little did I know, I would soon be given the chance to have my wish granted.

It was late October, Aubrey was entering her 3rd month on Earth, and you could say I received divine intervention while toiling at my latest part-time job site. I had just finished eating lunch with my three co-workers: Ron, an irritable sort with acne pockmarked cheekbones buried beneath a heavy beard; Bill, a slender, music-loving savant whose favorite pastime was listening to Casey Kasem's weekly countdown show, "American Top 40"; and Mickey, the simpleton of the group, who was nicknamed 'Doomy' by the others in the group because all of his sentences seemed to begin with "Do me' a favor…" Our quartet was charged with constructing a new strip mall along the town's main corridor, Highway 220, by our boss, Christopher Johnson. Chris was a burly, intimidating man with piercing blue eyes who wore flannel, which had him resemble a perfect blend of Paul Bunyan and Lex Luther from Superman. I took great pleasure when teasingly referring to him as the 'Troll'- especially when I would dare to say it right to his face. The 'Troll' and I got along quite well, though the rest of the construction crew considered Chris a huge asshole.

Most who knew me well would probably say that I have an easygoing personality. It was pretty easy for me to get along with everyone.

Of course my strong work ethic was a huge benefit to my healthy relationship with the boss. It was because of my reputation in the town that gave me the confidence to stride over to a local business owner who was obviously in distress, and having a difficult time controlling his anger over what appeared to be some recent bad news.

"Is there something I can help you with?" I asked, hoping to muffle the stranger's profanity-laced monologue. The business suit attired man began to look and me with suspicion, then contempt.

"Yeah" was the sarcastic reply, "if you can fork over thirty-five hundred dollars, the rights to my Subway franchise is yours!"

It quickly became obvious to me that the stranger's ability to open a sandwich shop in Oakhurst had been made impossible by his scorned wife's demand for a divorce. And somehow, at the end of his infuriated rambling, I surprisingly answered with a resounding, "Yes!" The stranger was equally surprised at how easy it had been to find someone willing to give him back his initial investment.

Opening a dining establishment had always been a deep down dream of mine, but I could never muster up the courage or know-how to pursue. You know, I didn't even have the guts to share that dream with anyone. Not Gil or Shelley or Rachel. I think it was out of fear that someone would laugh in my face and shatter my dream. While I had imagined owning and managing a more "fine dining" experience, a fast-food outlet made for a great substitute. Coaxing Rachel, though, would likely be the hardest part. Yet it wasn't hard. I won her over by the excitement and dedication I had for the idea, and the hours I would spend making the restaurant a success.

"Why not?" she thought, "At least it would make the rest of the town's female population safe from Rick's advances." Rachel was not ignorant of my extra-marital fantasies. She noticed how I would check out every person with a vagina, and this business venture might be the distraction we both needed.

For a brief period, the sandwich shop proved frustratingly just out of reach, as the thirty-five-hundred-dollar investment wound up harder to come by than originally thought. So I took this problem to Dad, reluctantly. I wanted to do this on my own and without any help from him. Surprisingly, he told me that there might be another option. Approximately ten years earlier, the family business had invested in a bottling plant that they had helped build in northern California.

Dad was able to sell their percentage for nearly half a million dollars, providing every member of our family a $100,000 stipend.

Rachel and I couldn't hide our happiness. Of course Elfrieda, in her typical childish manner, managed to place a slight damper on the excitement by throwing me an uncalled-for snipe, "I'm guessing that now that you have too much money, you'll be sure to rub it in our face every day." It took plenty of effort to bite my lip and take the high road, refusing to dignify her self-loathing with a response. However, getting Wally's sign of approval always seemed to be what Rachel needed to proceed, and he was more than happy to provide that.

But money wasn't the only obstacle in obtaining the Subway franchise. There was also a two-week business course that we were required to take on the east coast, in the state of Connecticut. Rachel couldn't attend until Aubrey was old enough to forego breastfeeding, so we had to delay a bit. And of course when it was time to leave, we upset Elfrieda even further by placing Lindsay and Aubrey with my Mom and Dad back in Los Angeles.

Naturally, Rachel was extremely excited to learn that we would fly in to New York. She had never been to the Big Apple, and couldn't wait to tell everyone back home about her dreams coming true in the form of a gigantic shopping spree in Times Square. But she was disappointed that she didn't get to spend any time in Manhattan. When we exited the plane, we were greeted by a company representative at the JFK terminal, and quickly whisked north to the city of Milford, Connecticut. It wasn't too terrible a drive because our transportation was a cozy, stretch limousine. The vehicle had a big supply of complimentary booze. I figured it was a company perk that I was more than happy to take advantage of. Rachel didn't mind at first until, but became irritated when her slightly drunk husband made a clumsy attempt at a backseat seduction.

But it was my turn to become agitated when we appeared for the first day of orientation. Rachel was by far the youngest, and prettiest, woman in the training class of about 25-30. Because of this, she became the primary focus of the company's franchising instructor, Nick Trevino. The dumbstruck, early forty-something executive overtly flirted with Rachel, who, in my opinion and to my dismay, flagrantly flirted right back. I had never been the jealous type. Of course, this wasn't the first time I witnessed other guys and their hopes for a chance with Rachel.

But I just felt we had a big task at hand and no time for her flirty escapades. We should be approaching this without distraction. But after putting up with her clearly inconsiderate behavior throughout the fourteen-day training period, in which we were taught the proper way to slice meat, maintain state and local health codes, provide a welcoming atmosphere, etc. – I snapped.

"Damn it Rachel, we're here to get started on a successful business, and you're acting like a fuckin' whore!"

Taken aback by my outburst, she snapped back, "You're gonna lecture me on how to act professionally with the opposite sex? Don't make me puke."

"Hey, we're here to get a job done. Learn how to properly make a sandwich, run a business and make some money. Get with the program."

With that last statement Rachel became infuriated by the accusation of not pulling her weight, even more so than by the ass chewing about flirting with the instructor. She balled her hand into a fist and, with all her might, took a swing at me, hitting me flush in the face. The pain was excruciating and I was lucky that my nose was not broken.

"How dare you!", she screamed, "We're doing this together! So, don't accuse me of stepping out, asshole!"

With that firm insult, Rachel retreated to the bathroom of our hotel room and slammed the door behind her. From the other side, she yelled, "You can take the test yourself!"

Bleeding profusely from my right nostril, that was the last thing I wanted to hear. As much grief as I had given Rachel for her carefree spending and lackluster skills around the house, I knew that without Rachel, there was no chance we would be given approval to open up the franchise. I knew apologizing alone would not be sufficient. I had to grovel a little and concede to Rachel's wishes as to which direction we would take our sandwich shop in regards to the design. After the initial excitement in purchasing the franchise, we had been at odds on this aspect and there was no sign of compromising on anything.

Somehow and ultimately, together, we were able to pass the test. But after that trip, the level of this love/hate relationship had now reached an all-time high. This was clearly not the best way to engage in a fresh new business venture.

18
SANDWICHES

The trip back to Oakhurst was quiet and uneventful. Literally. Rachel and I didn't say a single word to one another throughout the entire five-hour plane ride and subsequent four-hour road trek home. In past arguments, I was the spouse who had to say 'sorry' first, but after being punched in the face, this time I swore that I wouldn't. But after nine hours of no words at all, not even the radio, I couldn't stand the deafening silence anymore. Yep, I ate some crow and tried to be the bigger person. My apology tasted a little like red wine left out for a few days. Nevertheless, I had my reasons.

I vowed to get revenge, and did so during the construction of the sub shop. Since my buddies were in charge of the strip mall's development, I would be making the decisions and calling the shots in the building from the ground up. But I knew Rachel wouldn't stay away from the building for long, so my devious side took over. I got together with Troll to always make sure there were two sets of blueprints in the office, a customized, false schematic to show Rachel and to appease Elfreida that incorporated the two ladies' (constantly changing) minds, and then the real one. For the first time since the beginning of Milford, Rachel and I were satisfied. I didn't care if the foundation for it was based on some harmless deception

However, there was one tenant who wasn't happy with what he called favoritism towards me. Edward Anderson, owner of Eddie's Steakhouse, was opening the new strip mall's main attraction. Eddie's restaurant occupied the largest space- more than twice the square footage of the dozen or so small surrounding outlets. Yet, my shop, although I guess I should say "our" shop, was completed and ready to open even before

Eddie's plumbing had passed inspection. But there proved to be a hefty price to pay for this favoritism. I promised Ron, Troll and the other guys complimentary sandwiches when the franchise opened.

During the time of the restaurant's construction, I did form a tight bond with Troll. He was the only member of the crew who wasn't married. This meant that Troll was always available when I wanted, or needed, a night away from Rachel. Troll was also the perfect cover-up whenever my dear old mother-in-law came over. Elfrieda's late model Chevy had a broken passenger-side headlight and a terribly loud engine with a knock that could be heard for miles. This gave me plenty of time before Elfrieda parked out front to call Troll with an escape plan. Troll would redial me in ten minutes with some kind of emergency plea for help. Sure, Rachel thought something was suspicious about the number of times I would leave home to help my supervisor, but she never connected that they timed perfectly with her step-mother's arrival. My devious side, once again.

In the days before the sub shop's early spring opening, we played host to family visitors. Rachel was given plenty of help with the kids from her sister Lindy and, of course, Mom and Dad. Having my parents help was made possible by me convincing Dad to rent a small, two-bedroom condo in the neighborhood for six months. Mom, who considered herself a city gal through and through, even at middle age, wasn't in love with the idea. But it did give her plenty of time with Lindsay and Aubrey. By the time the health inspector approved the restaurant's license, the town of Oakhurst had two more "temporary" citizens with the surname Martinez.

As hard as I tried, I just couldn't sleep the night before the grand opening. I couldn't turn off my mind. It was racing with a mixture of feelings. Excitement. Nervousness. Apprehension. And as much as I hate to admit it, the somewhat yearned for approval from Dad. I drove the two and a half miles from our house to the shiny new diner sometime after two o'clock in the morning, where I sat out front, just staring at the shop's sharply painted façade. I felt a sense of great pride and accomplishment unlike any other. I was finally a true entrepreneur, with a business all my own. We were so filled with anticipation of the business that Rachel and I customized the license plates on our vehicles. Hers read, Subwy4U. Mine read, 4USubwy. I also fantasized about making enough money to buy a string of franchises, maybe every

Subway in the county. I spent more than an hour sitting alone in my truck gazing at the storefront before heading back home.

The Grand Opening was scheduled for 10:00 a.m., yet Rachel and I, along with all of our close family members arrived before eight. The three employees Rachel had hired appeared within five minutes of their scheduled 9:00 a.m. clock in. I fired up the ovens, toasting the different styles of bread and cooking the deli meat to brand specifications, while Rachel prepared the condiments display, supervising the slicing and dicing of herbs and vegetables. Naturally, Mom purchased the first sandwich before the doors were unlocked. Corny or not, we framed the first dollar, which would hopefully be the first of many.

At 10:00 a.m., my worst fears began to take hold. There was no one waiting at the front door. Hundreds of cars rushed passed on the highway, but none bothered to stop. Elfrieda looked over with a bit of satisfaction at my restlessness. She always enjoyed watching others fail, but was especially ecstatic whenever it came to her son-in-law. She didn't care if Rachel happened to be collateral damage. Elfrieda's smile dimmed slightly when the shop's first customer entered about twenty minutes past the hour, and her grin disappeared completely as one patron after another followed.

By 11 a.m., the relatives were pushed out the door, where a line of hungry customers had continued to form. At that time, I was happily forced to return to the backroom to prepare more bread and meat. As the only franchise besides McDonalds in the town, the line at Subway would be an everyday fixture for an entire year. The deli was so busy that Rachel had to work seven days a week as cashier, and Mom came out of retirement to help make sandwiches. There wasn't even time to interview extra employees. Elfrieda did find a silver lining in our success in that she and Wally could tend to their grandkids all day.

By the end of September, Rachel was getting pretty tired of working so much, even though at this time she was spending a more manageable five days a week in front of the register. Gladly, I agreed to hire a replacement, as long as Rachel would handle the bookkeeping chores. Who's kidding who? I was not good with numbers, and was more than relieved to give the responsibility to somebody else. I might not have been so gracious had I known the influence Elfrieda and Rachel's new found religion had over her in regard to financial choices.

My own generosity was also tested in the fall. Construction of the other shops in the strip mall had been completed, yet Ron, Troll and the guys were still dropping by three or four times a week asking for a free sandwich. Even worse, they were cutting in line to get them. I finally had to put a stop to it. Only Troll remained a good friend from then on. That thirty-five-hundred-dollar investment seemed like a lifetime ago. Or perhaps I should say a lifestyle ago. That chunk of change turned into thirty-five hundred dollars a day of profit. I had finally arrived. And I relished in the envy of the people of Oakhurst.

The beautiful surroundings of Oakhurst, not to mention Mom and Dad, eventually persuaded Beth and her husband to move to town. The entire family, with the exception of Gil's family, were once again living within a few minutes of each other. In the form of a sandwich shop, it felt for a while like my ship had come in. However, the peaceful lull in our marriage due to our hectic schedule, was about to come to a bitter end.

19
COLLAPSE

After almost a year of seven-day workweeks, I was more than ready to enjoy the fruits of our labor. While I did grow tired of the free sandwiches taken by my buddies, I had no problem, and in fact, enjoyed the hand shake deal with the local golf pro. I gladly provided him free food in exchange for free rounds of golf, anytime. Never did I ever think I would love the game so much. I wasn't any good but I loved to be out on the course. It seemed like every weekend, I was delivering a couple foot longs to the course and staying to play eighteen holes. Most of the time with Dad and Beth's husband and son, my nephew. There would also be times, perhaps on a slower Tuesday where I would pick Lindsay up from school, drop her off at Mom and Dad's, and play a quick nine on a perfectly golden afternoon. In Los Angeles, my "therapy" would be catching a five-foot swell at Zuma. In Oakhurst, first, it was reeling in a largemouth bass at the lake. Now, striping a golf ball down the middle of the fairway. During some of those weekday afternoons, there were times when I was the only one on the course. I had the entire place to myself. Hit a tee shot. Pop a top. Sink a ten-foot putt to save bogey. Another iced cold one. Sit in the golf cart and mentally count the thousands of dollars coming into the restaurant. It was as easy as counting the strokes on my scorecard. Early retirement began to creep into my mind.

But I was in for quite a shock when I innocently asked Rachel one day how much money was available in our savings account.

"Almost nothing," came the terse reply.

Unbeknownst to me, Rachel had been tithing over $300 a week to the local ministry; a gift to God for the wonderful bounty He had provided with the successful family business. Rachel had also been paying round-trip airfare from Missouri to California twice a year for Lindy's month long visits in spring and autumn. And of course, Rachel's daily shopping sprees had gotten out of hand once again. I didn't know it at the time and wouldn't find out until years later, but there was also the helping hand Rachel gave to her parents, who had insufficiently planned for their retirement. Not to mention the $35,000 that she so easily handed over to Wally to start his janitorial business that failed miserably. Wally and Elfreida's poor attempt at retiring was going to have a hand in delaying mine.

I was beyond irate at the news of our non-existent savings. It took everything I had not to reach out and strangle the smug look off her face. Rachel appeared almost proud of fucking me royally, and not having to take me to bed to do it. It didn't seem to matter that she managed to screw up her own plans of adding an extra bedroom and bathroom to the house.

It was five minutes later before I could calm myself down enough to speak.

"You selfish bitch!" I somewhat cringed when using that phrase. To no surprise, Rachel hated to hear it. But I figured if there was ever a perfect time to utter the word to Rachel, this was it.

"What made you think that it was okay to spend all of my hard-earned money on yourself?!"

Rachel glared back at me before screaming, "YOUR hard-earned money? Since when did it become YOUR hard-earned money? Did you forget that I slaved for six months at the stinkin' shithole, and I'm still working twenty hours a week keeping the books!"

I had to shake my head in amazement. Sarcastically, I began to clean my ears while trying to make sense of what I was hearing. This measly savings was Rachel's idea of keeping the books? So to try to talk some sense into her thick head, I tried to put a spin on Rachel's argument. "Okay, if that's the case, why wasn't I allotted any money for my sweat and tears?"

"You gave all yours away in free sandwiches to your friends!" Rachel sassed back.

"Really!!!" I snapped, "And how much do you figure that was?"

Rachel knew she would never get me to understand and threw up her hands. "You know you spend just as much as I do on stupid crap. There's your beer, your fishing trips with Troll, and"

I interrupted, "I haven't gone fishing in months. I'll tell you what we do…" I wanted to continue my thought but stopped and realized that I would be giving away my most effective mother-in-law escape scheme. "Aaah, forget it." But before I conceded, I needed to make one final and firm statement. "We are not giving any more money to the church! Now it's my turn to get paid! And I'm not working at the shop anymore to get it, either!"

A few days earlier, Troll told me that a new housing sub-division was going up across town, and the there was a huge need for a tiling expert. You see, tiling was the one job affiliated with construction that I really enjoyed doing. So that's when I decided that I was going to hand the daily operations of the sandwich shop to someone else. I would simply take the profit earned as the franchise's owner, while supplementing the family income with a new operation, my own business that specialized in the tiling process. However, in order to convince Rachel of the expansion idea, I knew I was going to have to let my monumental disagreement slide. The planned vacation I had been looking forward to with Rachel and kids was going to have to wait too.

In no time at all, I was granted the construction contract, and I began work immediately. Things were going great. However, a mere ten days into the job, I received an emergency phone message from Elfrieda,

"Rick, we need you at the restaurant now!"

When I arrived, I was surprised to find the restaurant was closed. I raced around to the back where I found Elfrieda waiting at the employee and delivery entrance. She was crying, and I couldn't even be happy about it.

"What's going on?" I asked with much concern.

Elfrieda wiped the tears from her face and with misplaced anger exclaimed, "The franchise supplier has refused to make a delivery for the last five days. And we've run out of food!"

I was shocked and puzzled, "You waited until now to tell me? Did you ask them why they've stopped shipment?"

Elfrieda replied, "They said something about you owing them $15,000. Maybe more."

"Wait a second", the words stammered out, "You and Rachel sign the checks. Why haven't you guys paid them?"

Again, Elfrieda was standoffish. "Because there's no money in the account to pay them."

I had never stopped to consider that once Rachel had run through the family's personal savings, she would go after the business account. I was absolutely infuriated. Another huge fight over financial problems ensued between Rachel and I. This time, I had no choice but to relieve Rachel of all financial responsibilities and take full control of the check book. When I called the franchise vendor, he explained that I needed to wire at least $15,000 into the company's account before they would ship anything.

At the bank, I removed Rachel and Elfrieda as signers of the sandwich shop account. And while I did get some looks of question and wonder that can only be found in a small town, fortunately I built the reputation of being a well-known, upstanding citizen in the community. So I was able to borrow the money with nothing but a handshake from the bank president. When Rachel found out that I was able to get fifteen grand with no collateral, she wasn't satisfied at all, replying, "Why didn't you ask for 20 thousand?"

Unfortunately, that wasn't the end of our family's financial problems. Rachel's credit cards were all maxed out and the bills were piling up. To make matters worse, I stumbled across several unopened letters from the I.R.S. while sorting through Rachel's unfinished paperwork mess. She had never bothered to pay the sandwich shop's employee payroll taxes. I tried to work the numbers over and over, but I realized that the only way for me to get out of this huge pile of debt was to sell the franchise outlet.

Rachel was horrified when I relayed this information to her, "You're going to embarrass me in front of my friends. I told them I had taught you how to properly maintain the accounting books."

Now it was my turn to be horrified by what I was hearing. I chose to ignore it, as if I were mentally blocking out the pain of a deep cut. The once strong love I felt for Rachel was quickly floating away like a dissipating cloud. It was actually turning into a deep hatred.

Once I decided to sell the franchise and thought that financially things would start turning around, another major mistake, one I had made, had caught up with me. Somehow I had failed to report capital gains on the house we sold in Los Angeles. If Rachel and I wanted to keep our house in Oakhurst, we would have to fudge on our taxes. Desperate times called for desperate measures. However, Rachel, whose Christian faith had grown stronger over the years, refused to lie. Although the decision was morally correct, it didn't excuse her amoral behavior toward me. The pain I felt when my childhood dog Rags died was nothing compared to the day I was forced to give up the house that I cherished so deeply. This was the house that Rachel and I were supposed see Lindsay and Aubrey grow up in. It was our dream home. At the beginning, this house had seen such happy times and promise of good cheer. Now it was nothing more than a punch in my gut. I was nothing short of devastated. Not just devastated with the loss of the house and the restaurant, but my tiling business also came to a screeching halt due to the hit my credit took. And to top it off, I was still $250,000 in debt to state and U.S. governments. I was devastated that I was now in a position where it felt like I had nothing to show for what I had accomplished in my adult life.

And while Rachel did regret some of the financial decisions she made that put us in this position, not once did she regret purchasing the thousands of dollars of gold, silver, and platinum trinkets that she had packed up tight in her rather expansive jewelry box that I knew nothing about. Sure, the kids would now have to share a small bedroom in our small, broken-down rental just down the street from our dream home, but they'd always be able to say that their mother looked like a million bucks. And to make matters worse, Rachel so kindly sprung on me as we moved the last of our belongings into that tiny house, that we would be welcoming a son in a little more than five months.

While I should have been thrilled with this news, I was unable to take much solace in it with the recent events. And while Rachel spent her Sunday's at church praising God for all of the blessings in our life, I could not understand why her Loving God would make me lose everything I worked so hard for. But at least I could find a blessing in our son.

When Luke was born in early December, our marriage had become at least bearable. This was mainly because I wasn't home at all during the day. I picked up a job working outside the city, and away from Rachel, Monday through Friday, and spent the weekends building Dr. Melbourne's winter chalet in exchange for living rent free in his small cabin instead of paying for our rental. But things hit rock bottom for me shortly after New Year's Day. I had already sold my truck because we couldn't afford to make the final three payments, although I couldn't part with the license plate. I did manage to score a motorcycle as part of my trade-in, but riding to and from job sites in freezing rain and snow, I would spend the first 45 minutes at each destination trying to get warm enough to feel my fingers and toes. But I would survive. It was Luke who was diagnosed with pneumonia.

At the hospital, the doctors gave him only a 50% chance of making it through the night. When I heard this, I turned to my Mom, who had come for support, and buried my head into her shoulder. While I was breaking down, Rachel was furious that I wasn't comforting her. I saw her look over at Wally and Elfrieda and whine, "Please take me home, now. Rick and Helen obviously can handle this."

I heard Rachel leave, but I made no attempt to offer a goodbye. There was no way I would ever leave my precious son. What kind of parent would do that?

Thankfully, Luke did make it through the night, and after four days in the NICU, he was cleared to go home as soon as we completed CPR certification. Rachel, who already knew the life-saving procedure, received her certificate in a matter of minutes, but I had trouble with the course, and it took me nearly an hour before passing.

As soon as Luke was placed in the car seat in the back of Rachel's Jeep Cherokee, Rachel laid into me. "I can't take this anymore. I have to say it, Rick. You're worthless! You are a terrible father to your children! You're a bad businessman! And you're a rotten husband!"

I was dumbstruck. She was blaming me for HER fuck up! I drove home without saying a word, glancing only once over at Rachel, who looked rather pleased with herself as she listened to her gospel music.

After returning home, Rachel pulled Luke from the back seat. She noticed that I hadn't shut the engine off, or made any attempt to get out of the car.

"Aren't you coming?" she asked.

"No," I said. "I'm going to take a drive. I need a few minutes to myself."

"Suit yourself," she responded, as she slammed the car door and headed inside.

I took off down the slick road, not caring about the danger I was putting myself in, or possibly some innocent bystander. I only had 20 bucks left in my pocket; an arrogant, alienating wife at home; and no future prospects. No one would care if I died, right?

Just then, a fox with its three babies trailing behind it suddenly appeared in front of me. I swerved, but the tires locked up and the car began to skid out of control. The automobile missed the smallest cub by less than a foot and slammed into a five-foot snow embankment created by a road-clearing plow.

After collecting myself for a moment, I exited the vehicle slightly dazed, but caught a glimpse of the last of the fox family as it disappeared into the woods. My thoughts of suicide changed into memories of my own children.

"I've got kids who need me" I had an epiphany. "I can't kill myself. I have to make sure they don't ruin their lives like I've done." I looked up at the heavens and thought, "Why not? If it helps Rachel, I might as well try it". I fell to my knees in the middle of the icy road in the freezing cold and prayed. "Please God, help me out of this mess."

20
AFTERSHOCK

If God answered that prayer, it was not exactly the answer I had anticipated. It came in the form of a major earthquake in my hometown, Los Angeles. Because of this, billions of dollars were made available for the rebuilding of the City of Angels as quickly as possible, and our family's construction business was among the companies best positioned for an extremely large payday. The firm had already been working on the expansion of a major aerospace company, which would be used to fulfill top-secret government contracts. This connection put Martinez Construction at the front door after the trembler rocked the southland.

When Gil alerted Dad about the need to double the company's workforce immediately, Dad reached out to me. Within a few hours, I was packed and we were on our way to L.A. Even though I did not want to witness the devastation that altered life for many Angelinos, I didn't need to be asked twice. I packed one overnight bag, kissed my children goodbye, and gave Rachel a facetious wave.

Dad had always told the story about how he returned home from Korea after two years of fighting for our country. He was twenty years old and ready to start a life of his own. His ship docked in the bay area, where he got lucky enough to literally hitch a ride down the 5 freeway and walked through his door to no fanfare from any family or friends sometime around 3 a.m. Four hours later, he was on the job, earning a wage, building a parking lot with his brother. I never understood that or appreciated that, until now.

Dad and I got into the San Fernando Valley by 3:30 p.m., and were put right into work. We wouldn't get our first break until three days later. Passable detours were needed around freeway bridges that collapsed. Temporary shelters needed to be built for those people whose homes were given a 'red card,' stipulating that the building was unsafe to enter, even to get personal items. FEMA needed covered areas in which they could deal with the quakes' many victims.

I crashed at Gil's house during my first overnight break, where I was able to contact my old buddy, Jerry. As nice as it was of Gil to offer his house, I needed to find someplace to stay where I wouldn't be under the watchful eye of my older straight-laced brother. Jerry was already sharing an apartment with a guy named Sergio, but he insisted that they would make room for me. Besides, the apartment was much closer to our primary rebuilding job site than Gil's house. I again packed my bag, and after completing another sixteen-hour shift, I headed over to Jerry's place.

I was really excited about getting to spend time with Jerry. It had been a half-dozen years, and I hadn't realized how much I had missed the red-headed party animal. I couldn't wait to unwind and let loose a bit when and if I ever got the time. These past few years with Rachel had been no cup of tea, and if it weren't for our kids, I'm not sure our marriage would still be intact. Let's be honest, I loved being far away from Rachel, and thanks to the recent turmoil in our relationship, I was able to get away with calling back to Oakhurst only once or twice a week. If it weren't for the kids, who knows how long I would have gone without phoning home.

When I got to Jerry's apartment, I was troubled to find that it was a two-bedroom residence. Even though I would have gladly crashed on the couch, Jerry insisted that I take his bedroom, saying he wouldn't mind sleeping on the living room couch.

"It's cool, buddy," assured Jerry, "You're gonna need some privacy when your wife comes to visit. Besides, I'm taking most of the closet space."

I smiled at that last remark. Jerry always had the perfect outfit for every event, and he always had a lot of different clothes to choose from. Not to mention his massive shoe collection. Although I felt badly about him giving up his room, I obliged. After a very hard work week, his bed was extremely comfortable and I was too tired to protest.

Because of the long hours, I made a lot of money working overtime. I sent Rachel only ¼ of my paycheck every other week, which was plenty to cover the family's expenses. I would put half in a checking accounting that I opened at a local bank, in my name only, with the rest used for paying rent, gas and also for the nightly partying alongside Jerry. Even though Dad, Gil and I continued to work sixteen-hour days, my adrenaline allowed me to spend four of the other eight hours at bars or catching up with old friends from the neighborhood.

After several months, with most of the city's heaviest damaged services in working order, my schedule became less hectic and my partying became more similar to the parties I had back in my bachelor days. The sunny skies and sandy beaches of Los Angeles could not be scarred by any fault zone, and I was surprised that I ever felt Oakhurst's mountains were a suitable replacement. Maybe it was because my domineering father had already headed back to his now retirement villa in Oakhurst, but southern California never looked so good to this San Fernando Valley native.

As much as I did not miss Rachel, and as much as I was living the life I had become accustomed to before we had kids, being without my precious children was becoming unbearable. I found myself calling home more frequently to talk to the children, and even made a few trips back to visit when I was able to break away from the job. On one particular trip, I gave Rachel the day to do what she wanted while I spent all day with the kids. We had lunch at the Pizza Factory, played arcade games there as well as at the bowling alley, in between a couple of games of bowling. The kids loved bumper bowling. Oakhurst that day was not what it had been to me before. For one, I was noticing the once friendly faces had now turned to dirty stares at me. I could almost hear the chatter under the breath of many but I couldn't quite make out just what they were saying. I could tell they were talking about me, and it didn't sound good. Finally, I took Lindsay to get her hair cut, but we were pretty much pushed out the door. The manager there mentioned they were booked. It was becoming painfully clear that I was no longer welcomed in that town.

Later that night, Rachel and I chatted before I needed to make the four-hour drive back to LA. She told me that Lindy had suggested that because I am out of town for work, perhaps Rachel and the kids should go spend time with her and her biological mother, Dottie, in Missouri. Lindy had assured Rachel that they could stay with her since she had extra room since Chad had passed, and she would love the company. And of course, she spoke highly of the amazing church that they were a part of. While I didn't think it was a terrible idea at first for her to spend time with Lindy, something didn't sit well with me when it came to her mother and the church. I couldn't imagine that Dottie, who left Rachel and her siblings as children to go be a part of this "amazing" church, would be a good influence for Rachel, nor would she have any love for her grandkids seeing as she was so quick to disregard her own children. By the end of the conversation, I had made a decision.

In the eight months I had been away from Oakhurst, I decided it was time to make the move permanent. Less than three years removed, Subway seemed like a lifetime ago. I didn't miss nature at all. I couldn't get far enough away from Elfreida. And most of all, I missed my kids. As soon as I got back to L.A., I started looking for an appropriate apartment for Rachel, the kids, and I.

As soon as I found a place, we were set to make the move. As I pulled up to Dr. Melbourne's snow-covered rental, home to my wife and kids, I wasn't focused on the picture perfect scenery I was leaving behind, but the smallness of the two-ton truck that held the entire contents of the family's belongings. We used to have a fully furnished two-story house with three acres of land, and now, all that we had left, fit easily into the back of a used vehicle. The silver lining, though, was leaving with no heavy debt load. I had set up an easy payment plan to pay back everything we owed within a five-year period, and had built up a nice little savings because I was controlling the finances.

Rachel, for the first time, showed a bit of gratitude towards me. She discovered in my absence just how much work it was raising three little ones. Sure, Lindsay spent most of the weekdays attending grade school and Aubrey was busy in pre-school, but when I wasn't around to help take care of Luke, that young boy was a handful. So much so that Elfrieda refused to look after him for more than one day a week, usually on Sunday. She chose that day because that allowed Rachel to go to church and mingle with the other members of the congregation.

The preacher listened to Rachel's complaints about her uncaring husband, before suggesting counseling for us. Rachel suggested it to me as a way to find a solution to our problems, and she was relieved when I agreed that we should see someone. Of course I agreed, because I knew that all the problems were Rachel's fault. And besides, now that we were going to be living together again, we should try to make it as civil as possible.

Within a couple of days of settling in our apartment in Northridge, Rachel politely asked me if she could take control of the finances again. I firmly stopped her in her tracks, but not without adding, "Maybe a little later. Let's see how frugal you are in furnishing the kids' rooms."

We still had our own bedroom set, along with a dining room table, a couch, a few chairs, a refrigerator and a stove; which we were able to keep during the Oakhurst garage sale. I was pleasantly surprised that Rachel didn't put up much of a fight over the checkbook.

When I was leaving for work the following morning, Rachel had pulled out the local yellow pages and thumbed her way to the letter 'C'. She flipped opened to the pages with the largest list of churches and closed her eyes. "Dear God, point me in the right direction. Show me where our family needs to go to receive your blessed healing." With that, she circled her right hand above the directory for a few seconds before quickly lowering her index finger down to the middle of the left side of the book. Rachel opened her eyes, and with a satisfied smile exclaimed, "Lily of the Valley' is our new place of worship."

I really wanted the marriage to work, even if it was only for our children's happiness. And while I was a bit troubled by Rachel's belief that God personally picked the church the family was to attend, I reluctantly agreed to give it a shot.

The drive to the chapel offered a pleasant panoramic view of the valley. The church was nestled in the northern foothills. But when we got to the holy grounds, I was absolutely appalled to discover that it consisted of a double wide trailer, stationed in a small, dirt-filled clearing. There was a second, smaller trailer that was used as an office and nursery.

There were only twenty or so people who attended the service. When the pastor arrived to give his sermon, I thought I recognized the middle-aged man, but couldn't remember where I had seen him. Three minutes into his fire and brimstone tirade, the pastor began speaking in an unusual language. His devoted followers, and Rachel, stood up, raised their hands to the sky and started yelling, "Hallelujah!"

The pastor also nudged me to rise, and I got the distinct whiff of alcohol. "That's where I know him!" I thought, "He's one of the regular barflies at the Candy Cat" which was an adult club that I had frequented back in my bachelor days. When Rachel saw the surprised look on my face, I am sure she assumed it was because I had never heard someone speak in tongues before. That was correct, but really I just wasn't buying into it. I thought the whole thing was ridiculous. This guy was selling the fact that God spoke through him every Sunday, while the rest of the week he was stepping out on his wife!

After three visits, I refused to continue with what I considered was a charade. I was especially angered that the pastor had begun to take an added interest in Rachel. When I brought this up to Rachel, the reaction was much calmer than our time in Connecticut for Subway with the franchise instructor. This time, she just laughed, telling me I was imagining things.

I responded with "It takes a player to know a player, and that guy is a player who has the hots for you! I'm sick of this shit. I'm not going to church and watch some pervert undress you with his eyes. The kids are going with me to the mall. You can have your snakes and tambourines…"

Rachel stammered, "Well that's just fine with me, but next week, we are going to get some counseling just like you promised!"

"Fine!" I snapped back. "Are you gonna let God pick that one out for us too?"

Rachel's only answer was to slam the door behind her as she headed for church. I looked over at our children. The two girls smiled back, while Luke let loose a loud fart. They all seemed quite content without Rachel around. "Come on kids, we're going out!"

When I returned home with the kids, I found Rachel watching a televangelist named Danny Hawn, who was extorting his flock to send him as much money as they could afford, and even more-so. Rachel's hands were clasped as if in prayer, and she ignored my sarcastic comment, "You listen to him for guidance, I'll listen to Howard Stern!"

I couldn't help but let out a loud laugh my own witty comment. I was about to turn my attention back to the kids when I noticed Rachel crying. Feeling slightly guilty, I snuggled up to her and whispered, "I'm sorry, baby. I didn't realize how much this stuff really means to you."

Rachel looked up at me with pleading eyes, "Pray with me?"

While I thought this was ridiculous, I thought this was a chance for me to get some extra loving tonight so I obliged, "If you believe that'll help…"

Rachel nodded. I got down on my knees next to her as Rachel began, "Oh Heavenly Father…" and continued to ramble in prayer.

After about three minutes, I was unable to withstand the hypocrisy and interrupted Rachel, "And dear God, please tell her to shut the fuck up because my beer is getting warm and I'm missing the Howard Stern Show."

A pissed-off Rachel yelled, "You sonofabitch! I can't believe you!"

I quickly responded sarcastically, "Uh, Oh! God's gonna punish you for saying that!" With that, I got up, leaving Rachel in the living room alone. "What an asshole", she screamed.

Not shockingly, that was also Rachel's comment about the marriage counselor after one meeting. First of all, Gina Dragoo, was a female. Secondly, after Rachel and I gave our mismatched assessment of each other, Gina seemed to be more on my side, telling Rachel that she was in love with the idea of a marriage and not being a wife. I also took a hit for my selfishness, which I owned up to. But Rachel refused to believe that she was wrong at all. She also laughed at the idea that she may be suffering from post-partum depression or bipolar disorder. She felt that was absurd, and that was the first and last counseling session we ever attended.

Despite our rocky re-start in Northridge, we surprisingly were able to settle down and live in peaceful tranquility for the next six months. Rachel stopped pushing me to join her as a member of the radical church up the hill, and I tolerated coming home to find her asleep in a messy house with a trio of hungry kids. And against my better judgement, after multiple times of her asking, I gave Rachel the responsibility of managing the checkbook.

In doing so, Rachel discovered that I had a separate checking account that was in my name only, and that I hadn't been giving her all of the money I was making for her to blow on shopping while she was still living in Oakhurst. This sent her into a spiral of rage, and she decided to go to church to pray about it. I took off to the local bar to have a beer, and to let her cool off.

When I returned home I found a ghastly-looking Rachel. Her light blue eyes had turned jet black, and her stare was as cold as ice. She hissed at me, "I can't stand this. I don't love you anymore."

Rachel picked up her ten-inch thick Bible and waved it at me. "Every time I look at you I see serpents coming out of your head!"

"Yeah, yeah. If you are so unhappy, there's the door!" I said sarcastically. I was exasperated and exhausted. "But I'm sleeping in my own bed. If you're afraid my monstrous snake will bite you, sleep on the couch." I walked down the hall and into the bedroom, closing the door behind me. I slowly undressed, waiting for Rachel to join me. After a few minutes, I realized she wasn't going to come in. Elated, I fell to my knees and prayed to God, "Thank you, a night of freedom, peace and quiet!" Little did I know I would soon find out just how much that freedom was going to cost me.

21
PANIC

Monday morning with a loving wife and family can be a wonderful start to the work week. You roll out of bed with the sun pouring a welcoming beam of light through your bedroom window. When it's a nice, hot shower with the water pressure just right bursting out of that shower head, perhaps you buy an extra minute or two under that serenity. Throw a towel around your waist and enjoy some music from the radio or perhaps some Rick Dees in the morning while carefully addressing that clean, close shave. Then, you stroll downstairs, say good morning to the kids and have some sort of warm breakfast. Finally, you kiss someone goodbye, wish them a good day, load the little ones in the car, drop them off at school before beating the traffic to work. That hadn't been my Monday for a long time. Today was no exception.

The alarm clock buzzer sounded like a warning to the city. It took much effort to roll out of bed and into the cold shower. Rachel must have been really late paying the water bill. One of the many hiccups since she took over the money again. Checking the clock, I cut myself shaving and rushed downstairs, nearly breaking my back tripping over one of Luke's toys. Rachel was feeding the baby. One less thing to do. Scarfed down some cold oatmeal. Then, I had to referee the umpteenth sisterly argument between Lindsay and Aubrey, all the while combing their hair and putting their clothes on so Rachel could take them to school. I anticipated Rachel was going to keep me an extra fifteen minutes repeating the same sermon she had heard the day before. To my surprise, she all but pushed me out the door, not even asking me what time I would be home from work.

I had trouble concentrating on the job. You see, I wasn't entirely ready to be a single man again. I was guiltlessly having thoughts of other women and wondering if the grass was truly greener on the other side. Eventually those thoughts would fade away in favor of those three smiling faces to greet me when I walked through the door after a long day of back breaking work.

Somehow, I made it through that Monday and as I jumped in my car, I had a great idea. I would get home, kiss Rachel the way I kissed Rachel when we were dating, hug my kids and tell them we were going out to Sizzler for dinner to celebrate absolutely nothing and everything all at the same time. I didn't know what the future had in store for our family, but I did come to the conclusion that Rachel and I should give it one more try. I was ready to love her like I used to, when our love was brand new. I raced onto and off the freeway. My Love by Little Texas was the song on the radio as I pulled into the bank to withdraw some money for our "special" evening. I might have been a little giddy, even sharing with the lovely bank teller these fun plans for my family this Monday evening. However, the bank teller slammed the door on my plans as if she was locking it shut and throwing away the key.

"Mr. Martinez, I'm sorry, but there is no more money left in this account."

"That's impossible! There must be a mistake. Not that you're the one making a mistake but can you please check again?"

"It shows a zero balance, Mr. Martinez."

"I had my wife deposit over six thousand dollars on Friday. How can there be nothing left?"

Then, a gravely sickening feeling shot through my suddenly cold body. And before I could continue, "It looks like Mrs. Martinez withdrew more than twenty-three thousand dollars earlier today. I'm sorry sir. There is nothing left."

I didn't even hear the last words. Somehow I got back in the car, raced home, pulled in the driveway and as I walked through the front door, it was all there for me to see.

I ran up the stairs yelling at the top of my lungs. "Rachel! Girls!" Opened all the bedroom and closet doors. The luggage was gone. "Where are you?" Ran back downstairs and out to the back yard and patio area. And while I wish I was hearing Luke scream, it was just me. "Please! Tell me where you are!" I stormed back inside and to the kitchen. I looked for a note on the fridge or the counter. I knocked over a few dishes hoping to find anything. It started to become clearer. I could feel myself slow down, stammering to the living room. The place was a mess. Couch cushions all over. Clothes thrown left and right. Coffee table and end tables were moved. It looked like a robbery. It felt like a robbery. I dropped to my knees. Then lying flat on the floor, I saw a piece of paper under the couch. A note. It was in Rachel's handwriting. But it wasn't to me. It read, *"Lindy, Joplin Airport, gray suburban, 8 p.m. sharp!"*

I crawled over to the phone and tried to dial seventeen phone numbers all at once. It took me five minutes to finally get one right.

"Mom. It's me."

"What's wrong, mijo?"

"I think Rachel kidnapped the kids. I think she flew to Missouri. She cleaned out our accounts. The kids' clothes and luggage are gone."

I heard the phone drop. A few seconds later, Dad was on the line. "Stay by the phone. I'm calling Bernie and I'll be down as fast as I can." Click.

Then, silence. Never had I heard a room go so quiet. It was wailing like a freight train in the middle of a restless night. Oddly enough, I went to the drawer and found a calculator. There are fourteen thousand, four hundred seconds in four hours. That's how long it was going to take for Dad to drive from Oakhurst to here. Fourteen thousand, four hundred seconds. What could I do while I waited? My body began to shake. I went to the fridge and opened up a beer. My hand shook so much I dropped the bottle after one sip and it shattered. Glass shot all over the kitchen floor. I grabbed another beer and drank it down.

Starting to think a little clearer, I checked the messages on the answering machine, hoping for some sort of explanation from Rachel. That weird little voice blurted, "You have three new messages. First message…"

"Hi, this message is for Rick Martinez. This is Roger from Pacific Bell. We haven't received a payment in over sixty days. It is imperative you address your past due notice to avoid cancellation."

Beep!

"Hey Rachel, this is Gail Allen from Lily of the Valley Church. You have always been so generous in the past with church fundraisers and we were counting on you to do so again. Let us know what we can expect from you. Thanks."

BEEP!

"Mr. Martinez, this is Chuck from the Department of Water and Power. We have sent three notices in the mail. If we don't get a payment by the end of the month, we will turn off your water."

BEEP!!!!!!

It seemed like the beeps kept getting louder. I was absolutely stunned. I decided to feed on an already half eaten cheese pizza, still in the box from two days ago. It was cold and rotten. I looked at the clock. Ten minutes had gone by. Six hundred seconds.

Another beer. Another message. Another stranger telling me my life was falling apart. And then...

"You have no more messages...BEEP!"

22
EPIPHANY

If ever there was a time for self-medication, this was it. I returned to the living room with two six-packs under my arm. When I found the TV remote amongst the still ransacked home, I turned it on and found the station set to Reverend Danny Hawn's program asking viewers to send him as much money as they could, and then even more. For every dollar they pledged, he would guarantee that they would sit at the right hand of the Lord, hundredfold.

"So this was the bullshit that had brainwashed Rachel" I realized. Some uncharted feeling came over me. So I picked up the phone and dialed the hotline that was keyed across the bottom of the TV screen. The young lady who answered was greeted with an unfortunate stream of obscenities.

"How the fuck do you people sleep at night, conning innocent people out of their life savings? You assholes are fuckin' leeches! You have destroyed my marriage, and if I'm ever able to find my kids, I'm going down to your fuckin' rich-ass studio and banging down the door of your satanic worshiping leader." I then hung up before waiting for an answer, surprised that the chick on the end didn't hang up first.

I still wasn't satisfied. I rifled through my personal address book and found Dottie's number. No one answered. Next, I had to call Rachel's father. Both Wally and Elfrieda were shell-shocked by what their daughter had done, and surprisingly, even Elfrieda pledged her support for me. Then I dialed Lindy's number. No one answered there either.

After finishing off my twelfth beer, I stumbled into the bedroom. Just as I pulled the covers over me, the phone rang. It was late. It had to be Rachel! I grabbed for the phone. "Rachel?!"

"No, it's Dottie."

"Where's Rachel? I have to talk to her."

"She's okay Rick" said Dottie calmly and sweetly. Her demeanor didn't change as she continued. "Rachel is such a trooper. I'm so proud of her. The kids are fine. She's fine. God bless you." And with that Dottie hung up.

"Motherfucker!" I shouted and got up to find the address book. I quickly dialed Dottie back. No answer. I dialed again. No answer. I tried five more times, out of desperation. It was no use. She had disconnected her line for the night.

"Why God? Why are you favoring arrogant, hypocritical sinners over a hard-working decent guy like me? This is fuckin' unbelievable!" I screamed while shaking my fist at the ceiling. I was way too infuriated to sleep at all that night. Those seconds kept ticking away. I could literally hear the second hand on the clock slowly circling. The tick, tick, tick somehow became a bang. Then a louder bang. After about ninety seconds of banging, I shook myself. It was the front door.

"Dad." I cried out his name just like I have must have a thousand times as a scared kid looking for some sort of guidance from the man who always seemed to know what to do and how to do it. He looked me up and down, paused, and then responded.

"Shit, boy! You look terrible," in a disappointing and scolding way.

"Yeah?" I retorted while swaying back and forth in my drunken stupor, trying to focus on the solitary figure in front of me. "The two of you don't look so hot to me either."

He grabbed my hand and guided me to the dining room table. From there, Dad really started in on me:

"All of my life, son, I've watched you jump from one thing to another, always running full steam ahead and never waiting for anyone who lagged behind. First, it was with soccer, then it was with construction, then the sandwich shop then back to construction. Same thing with women. When one didn't work out, you said 'goodbye' and moved on to the next one, never willing to compromise or see things somebody else's way. You've been selfish your entire life. You're over thirty now and you've always gotten things to go your way."

There, I felt I had no choice but to interrupt, "Bullshit, Dad. I'm in this mess because I always let Rachel get away with murder. She got a fucking nose job. She got cars. I moved to Oakhurst because she wanted to. She got a new car whenever she wanted, even if it meant I went without. And I gave her the fucking checkbook because she wanted to control it."

"No." Dad cut me off, "You gave her the checkbook, because you didn't want the responsibility. You moved to Oakhurst only when it fit you, because you felt it would hurt me. You bought the damn fancy company truck only because it best suited you. Everything you've done is to make life easier for you. Nobody else. That's why Gil inherited the family business. I knew if things got tough, he wouldn't give up and try something else."

"Great pep talk, Dad. I'm glad you know me so well. Maybe you could have told me earlier that Rachel was gonna clean me out."

Then, he screamed at me in a way I had never heard him scream at me before. "Damn it, Rick! She told you that three years ago with the sub shop!" He paused briefly before continuing. "I came over to see if you're ready, now, to do the right thing... for your children... OUR grandchildren. Do you really believe that Rachel has those kids' best interest in mind? They need their father. And like it or not, you ARE their father. Promise me, after you sober up, you'll do something about them? Please?"

Dad didn't wait for an answer. He left knowing that I was too emotional at that moment to provide a clear answer. He also figured I was minutes from passing out. Once again, he was right.

The next morning, I moped about in the condo. My only connection to the outside world was when I called every company and every agency Rachel and I had owed money to, asking for a few more days to get my affairs in order. Dad's harsh words echoed around my aching, throbbing head; a bitter lecture that no amount of drugs or alcohol could silence. But later that afternoon, there came an incessant ring from the intercom buzzer stationed perfectly in the hallway. At that time, I was in Luke's room, feeling sorry for myself. Normally, the fenced-in condo community was accessible to the entire public at all hours, since the front gate was always left open. I had been able to mute the sound of my life's failures and the belligerent thoughts in my mind by barricading myself in Luke's room. But when Dad left, he closed the front gate, forcing visitors to buzz to get in. There was no escaping the annoying chime anywhere in the house. The noise went on for fifteen minutes before I had to face the outside world.

Imagine my surprise when the person standing at my front door was…Beth! I was in shock to see my sister. She was the last person I expected at that time. She was holding what looked like a bag of groceries.

"Well? Aren't you going to ask me in?"

Snapping out of my daze, I replied, "Yes! Yes sis, of course." I was in no mood to see anybody, talk to anybody, or listen to anybody. But, I let her in anyways.

The first step in the door, Beth wrinkled her nose and gagged slightly as she got a whiff of the stench of cheap beer, stale cigarette smoke and my over-ripe body odor. The smell literally knocked her back a half-step. She quickly recovered and bravely moved forward, holding her breath and praying that I hadn't stashed Rachel's carcass somewhere inside. Beth set the grocery bag on the kitchen table and moved toward the closest window.

"You haven't killed her, have you? Cause I'm gonna kill her!" And I let out a loud laugh from the bottom of my belly. The first laugh in over twenty-four hours.

"You could use a little fresh air in here. Actually, this place needs a LOT of fresh air," Beth added as she moved about the condo, opening every window that she could find. After the fresh air was let in, she let out a satisfied, "There!" and headed back to the kitchen. "I made you some chicken soup. I'm guessing you're on the verge of malnutrition. And, I'm sure you could use a little home cookin', seeing that Rachel probably hasn't made anything edible in months."

I slowly shuffled my way to the table, sitting down where my sister had placed one of the serving bowls she had removed from the brown paper bag. She then pulled out a large container of soup and emptied a portion of the steamy contents into the bowl.

After pouring me soup, Beth handed me a spoon and sat down next to my grieving self. "Dad told me everything." She paused for a moment, "I have to say, you are one stupid ass motherfucker! How can you just sit here and do nothing while the wickedest witch in the world takes your children?!" She chose her words perfectly, considering I had always joked about her doubling as Miss Gulch.

"You have to stop thinking with your dick!" yelled Beth. I couldn't believe it. Actually, it sounded like something Shelley would say. However, it was more likely though, just a coincidence. After all, anyone who had said the same thing to me during the last twenty years would have been right.

I then had to state the obvious to Beth, "Boy, you must be dying to say 'I told you so.' You never liked her all that much, anyway."

"You're right, I couldn't stand her," came Beth's answer. "Here you were, ambitious, hardworking, and yes, never really had your priorities in order… until the kids came along. Many times I have seen the look in your eyes when you are with them or talking about them."

Beth let out a deep sigh before finishing her thought. "That's why I came here today. I wanted to look again at the man who would lay down his life for his children." She paused and then, "So, are you ready to go after them?"

I didn't know where to begin, and told Beth just that. "Bullshit!" she countered. "For years, you've been bitching about your wife, always complaining that she was just like her crazy biological mother. Didn't that woman run off to Missouri leaving behind two girls and a little boy who were at the very same age as your children are now? As they say, like mother, like daughter."

Beth was right. I had seen all the parallels between Rachel's arrogant life of entitlement and those of her 'real' mother- right down to the family make-up; the easygoing spouse who never could, or even cared to, meet the wife's impossibly high standards; and their warped moral compass instilled by an even more spiritual leader. Somehow, I never really noticed.

It was not until this point that I fully realized what Dad had been trying to tell me all along. I had never bothered to pay close attention to anything. That's why I allowed my money to disappear, twice. And that was why I failed to protect my children from Rachel's dangerous decline into religion. If anything bad should happen to Lindsay, Aubrey or Luke, it would be my fault, and my fault alone. This, I DID finally notice.

"Okay," I responded after my epiphany. "Let's get them back. First, I gotta call Dad and ask to borrow some money. I need to settle some past due bills. Then, I want to hire a private investigator to find out what else Rachel has planned or is planning."

"It's already been done" said Beth, as she pulled out the business card of a P.I. "He's already been given a retainer and is expecting your call."

I stared at the card that I'd been given. "How did you know what I was going to do? Wait. Don't answer that. Dad."

"Yep. Dad found the P.I. He also has Bernie on the job, ready to legally fight for the kids. I'm gonna straighten up around here while you make your calls. Let me know what I can do."

"One thing, Beth. Please, please don't wash the kids' clothes. Just put them all in Ziploc bags. I want to remember their scent in case I never see them again."

23
SEARCH

Bernie's small office typically opened at 9am, but he agreed to meet me at eight to figure out how we could get my kids back as quickly as possible. Of course I couldn't sleep a wink, so I showed up before sunrise and waited in my car for him to arrive. With the windows rolled down, I could feel the brisk spring air on my face. It was surprisingly refreshing, but also just cold enough to send chills down my spine. Or perhaps that chill came from the thoughts that were racing through my mind. Would we be able to find the kids? Were they really in Missouri? If Rachel is there, is she already brainwashed by her mother and Brother Scarborough? Would Rachel lie about kidnapping them and pretend she is only on vacation? Would she fight me about bringing them back? Would I ever see my kids again?

I finally heard a car pulling in next to mine at 7:59. That was just like Bernie, to be perfectly on time. He had always been reliable in past dealings with the family, so I had complete confidence that if anyone could help me get my kids back, it was him. As he was exiting his car with a friendly wave, I couldn't slow myself down. Without even as much as a simple "good morning," I began,

"I don't know how much Dad told you, but that bitch took my kids. I just know it in my gut that she is in Missouri with that psycho mom of hers and her mom's cult leader boyfriend. I'm ready to drive to LAX to jump on the next damn plane to bring my kids home. I called the P.I., but he said you already beat me to the punch."

Bernie Steinberg was a little, fragile man with a beak that looked like he would fit in our family. His demeanor was always calm and in control. He was methodical, in the way most great lawyers are, and he was the perfect balance for my scatterbrained and panicked personality. Bottom line, he had a heart of gold and my best interest at heart.

"Well good morning to you too, Rick."

That was just like him to make a simple comment to slow me down and bring me back to reality.

"I took the liberty of calling Scotty to work with him on his investigation to locate Rachel and the kids. He is on his way down there right now, and as soon as his flight lands, he will begin the search. He will be calling me to keep me updated. As soon as he confirms their whereabouts, we can begin drawing up the necessary paperwork to ensure we have the best chance to bring the kids home."

While this brought me a little comfort, I didn't like to hear him even suggest there was a chance I wouldn't get the kids back. But I did appreciate his honesty and that he kept me in the loop with the details of what was going on. And I couldn't help but chuckle a little bit at the thought of what Bernie's conversation with Scotty must have sounded like. Bernie spoke calmly, very matter of fact, and very much all business.

From the brief chat I had with Scotty, you could tell he was a Southern gem, who while very qualified, loved to bullshit and spoke in a very relaxed manner. He was a retired Texas Ranger, who spoke with a typical Lone Star State drawl. He had moved to L.A. to be closer to his grandkids, and therefore, had plenty of free time on his hands. Driving through the rural rounds north of Joplin, Scotty Smith would not be out of his element. He had spent some time in the Bible Belt south extraditing escaped criminals from the Texas hall of justice. He felt a sense of comfort in the towering wheat fields and wild grass that grew more than six feet high. Scotty was a veteran at rescuing kidnapped children, but unlike my case, ninety-nine times out of a hundred, the kids were taken by the father, not the mother.

Bernie continued, "By the way, when I spoke to Scotty this morning, he was just arriving at the airport. Rachel definitely flew somewhere, and she made sure to take the time to deflate your tires and leave your car on the top deck of the parking structure at LAX. So we will have to deal with that on our way out of town if we have to go pick up the kids. And by the way, did you happen to bring with you any photos of the kids?"

Looking for pictures of the kids had never been so agonizing. Pictures are kept for memories. Fond, wonderful memories. Never did I think I would have to look for pictures to give to an attorney because my kids were taken by my wife with the help of her mom and sister. Ironically, the first picture I had come across when looking was of Dottie. Also ironically, we got that picture from Wally and Elfrieda. If Wally had known how much shit Dottie talked about him, he probably would have thrown that one in the trash. Then we found the picture of Rachel and Lindy, arm and arm. I could picture them inside some church making that exact same pose while the kids were God knows where doing God knows what. And finally, as much as I didn't want to part with it, I gave Bernie our Christmas photo, the one where my precious little children smiled their biggest smiles in their matching red shirts. I then choked down the huge lump in my throat, and Bernie told me to head home for lunch and to meet back at his office in the late afternoon. By then, he assumed, Scotty may have some more information.

When I walked through the door, I was greeted with, "Rick, you should call the girls' school and let them know what's going on. You don't want Rachel calling them to try and get their records transferred."

Beth had just gotten back from grocery shopping. The place was pretty clean, thanks to my sister and now she had put some food back in the house. Mom and Dad were going to help me take care of the bills so I could keep the power on and make sure I was able to take a hot shower, which would be a blessing because taking evening runs had been the only way I had found to clear my mind, even in the weeks leading up to Rachel's disappearance. Somewhat embarrassingly, I had no idea just how much money I was in the hole. I got a whale of an answer when Beth got back from shopping. When she pulled into the garage, the car knocked over a few crates full of notices, letters, and so much paper that I had no idea where or how to start figuring out what it all was. Beth helped me sort the stacks of bills into a few piles. One pile was the stack of bills I had to address right away. The other piles, I knew I had some time.

Only a couple hours went by, but I just couldn't sit still. So I called Scotty again for an update.

"Rick, just as you thought. I was driving in my Ford Focus trying not to draw much attention. Sure enough, as I rounded a tree-lined corner, there appeared this housing trailer, with no place to seek cover for at least 100 feet. I carefully passed by the ramshackle abode and pulled into the driveway next door to this huge mansion. Brother Scarborough's mansion. I knocked on the door, just as I said I would, and the hick lady confirmed that the mansion was Brother Scarborough's place and that a lady named Dottie lived in the trailer. Said Dottie was being visited by some young Rachel with kids.' I'm on them Rick. As soon as I find out how the kids are, I'll call you back. Stay close."

"Ok great. Let me know how the kids look. Do they look healthy? I miss them."

"I know Rick. I'll do what I can. Talk to you soon,"

As soon as I hung up with Scotty, I called Bernie and fill him in.

"Bernie, I just spoke to Scotty and he said…"

"Rick, I know your mind must be going crazy right now but you have to let me discuss the details with Scotty. You have to stay out of this."

"Stay out of this? Bernie, those are my kids and…"

"Rick, I know. You just gotta trust me here. Do me a favor, don't come back to the office. Just pack a bag and wait for my call. When I call and say let's go, you have to be ready to go instantly. And Rick, this is extremely important, whatever you do, don't, under any circumstances, talk to anyone about anything. You got that?"

"Bernie, you're starting to scare me here. What do you mean?"

"Rick, again, please. I'm asking you to trust me. Scotty and I know what we are doing. And certain things gotta be done by the book. No exceptions. I gotta go." Click.

And with that, I felt put in a corner in pitch black darkness. How do I just sit and wait? How do I put the future of my life, and the lives of my children, in the hands of someone else? But I knew Bernie was adamant that I had to listen. So after I packed my bag, I sat and waited. And waited. And waited some more. The clock continued to tick by but time stood still for me. A few hours later, I decided to go for my evening jog around our neighborhood to clear my head. It kind of did me some good. It almost took my mind off of what was going on. However, when I turned onto the next street, it reminded me of the time I taught Aubrey how to ride a bicycle for the first time. I started running faster, until I got to a park where Lindsay would play with her friends after school. I started to think going for a jog was a bad idea. I didn't realize how much everywhere and everything would remind me of memories

I had with children. And it gets hard to run when you can't breathe or see because you are choking back tears and your eyes are so welled up that you can barely see through the blur.

When I got back from my jog, Beth had dinner waiting. Perhaps the first time in months that dinner was ready and waiting for me at home. Who cares if it was chili dogs and salad, it was food and I didn't have to cook it. I took two bites but I just couldn't eat. I was too sick to eat. So was Beth. We looked at each other, and without saying a word, we both knew what the other was thinking and feeling. And just before our eyes welled up with tears, I got up from the table and called Scotty again.

"Scotty, what do you know?"

"Rick, don't call me."

"I'm dying here Scotty. Give me something please."

"Ok. I found Rachel and the kids in town. Been tailing them for a few hours. The kids seem miserable but physically, they look ok. You can tell Rachel already feels like a queen. The people of Joplin absolutely love her. Nearly all of the church's 'younger generation,' those under the age of thirty, seem to be single women. Most of them have parents in the church. There are very few men in the town. After chatting with the gas station attendant, he told me that most of the male offspring tend to leave, either through marriage (and moving on to greener pastures in bigger cities), or by joining the military and having their horizons broadened to the point where small town life seemed so, well, small town. He also mentioned that there was a new good looking woman in town who all the young ladies have taken a liking to because she not only could teach them beauty and grooming tips, but also apparently gave a large donation to the church. He didn't say how much, but I knew that had to be her. That's how I found her."

He continued, "I saw them congregate at this park. It seems like they do this once in a while. I am assuming it is because Rachel has that major metropolitan history, which must be worshiped by the female disciples of the church. They seemed flock around her to hear what sounded like Rachel's stories of life among the rich and famous, along with the day-to-day dealings of the hustle and bustle of Los Angeles. Rachel is just eating up all the attention lavished upon her. I certainly didn't see Dottie or Rachel pay any attention to the kids, particularly Luke. Dottie seems all too happy to claim Rachel as her daughter because of all the attention it is bringing her. And the Brother I am sure is thrilled at the money that Rachel's presence is providing."

"Oh thank God you found the kids. And I can't believe that bitch used to cost me money and now she is making money for that satanic bastard," I snapped.

"Wait, Rick. It gets better. There is only one person I saw that did tend to the kids," he paused, "Lindy."

Well that was a shocker because Lindy always seemed depressed since Chad passed, and the times I saw her, she didn't even seem to be able to take care of herself let alone anyone else. I could only pray that she would do a better job looking after them than she did herself. With that, I thanked Scotty for the information and hung up to give Beth the update.

"Beth, you're not gonna believe this shit. Scotty says that Rachel has been anointed queen because of my money and because she knows how to comb hair. She's not even looking after the kids. Lindy is doing that."

Beth never cared for Rachel, and Beth had never been one to bite her tongue or hold back what she was thinking, "Those bitches better not hurt those kids. When you get the call from Bernie to head out, I'll buy my own plane ticket. Then I want you to lock me in a room with those two angels of mercy. I promise you they will get what's coming to them."

Beth and I chuckled a bit but really, the laughter was just masking my tears. I had yet to hear from Bernie, so against my better judgement, I decided to call Wally and Elfrieda to see if they had heard anything.

"Rick, you ingrate! You scumbag!"

That wasn't the greeting I was expecting from my supportive mother-in-law.

"Elfrieda, what the fuck are you talking about?" I snapped back.

"How could you Rick? Wally and I were on your side. We were gonna support you. Then, come to find out you've been beating her and the kids?!?!"

"What? Who told you that? That's bullshit."

"Doesn't matter Rick, we know..."

"You talked to Rachel?" I couldn't believe it. "When? What did she say? What are her plans?"

"Forget it Rick. You'll never see those kids again. I can't believe you molested Lindsay."

"You fat bitch. Your daughter kidnaps the kids, gives thousands of my dollars to some Brother Scarborough and now you're gonna believe that bullshit." Click.

Beth could see I was about to lose it. She handed me a beer and told me to call Bernie.

"Bernie, I just spoke to Elfrieda."

"What? Rick, what the fuck did I tell you? Don't talk to anyone."

"But Bernie, Rachel has been telling everyone I molested Lindsay and that I beat them all."

"Rick, enough! I'm gonna tell you one more time. Don't talk to anyone about anything. Just sit there and wait for my call. You cross me again Rick, I swear I'll call off this whole thing. Understand?"

"How am I supposed to do that? I can't just sit here."

"I don't know but you better figure it out. Just be ready when I call you. Goodbye."

I knew I messed up because I had never heard our mild-mannered, Jewish family friend swear like that. I tried telling Beth how Bernie expected me to just sit here and do nothing. How can a parent just sit around and hope for their kids to be found? My job as their father was to take care of them. Beth was doing her best to comfort me but I was just frozen. I was caught in a horrible combination of sorrow and helplessness.

"Rick, I know this is going to be easier said than done but try to get some sleep. When Bernie calls, not only do you need to be ready, but you need to be somewhat rested. Do it for the kids," she reasoned.

"Ok Beth, but please, if I don't hear the phone, please wake me up."

I slowly made my way up the stairs. Before I got undressed, I grabbed the guitar out of my closet. I took it to Luke's room and just began to play. Then, I stopped at the girls' room. I opened the door and began to play some more.

"Kids, if you can hear me, please hear this song. Daddy misses you. I promise we'll be a family again soon."

24
DESPONDENT

President John F. Kennedy was shot and pronounced dead in about thirty minutes. The Lakota tribe annihilated General George Custer's force in about an hour. The Titanic sank in less than three hours. And by now, it had been almost forty-eight hours since Rachel took the kids and exiled to Joplin, Missouri. And almost as bad, we knew where they were but still couldn't do anything about it. Bernie was still ironing out the details and the paperwork to make sure we were following procedure in this soon to be custody battle. In fact, he had me start writing a letter to the courts stating why Rachel had been an unfit mother and why I should get full custody of the kids.

At first, this assignment was humorous. Listing Rachel's shortcomings when it came to Lindsay, Aubrey and Luke was relatively easy. She was more interested in dressing herself than the kids. And she was way more interested in dressing herself in Gucci and gold. I could count on both hands how often she had prepared dinner for them. It was somewhat ironic that she had lied to Wally and Elfreida about me abusing her since she was the one who was extremely hard on Lindsay, almost berating her while helping her with homework. If you could even call it helping. Perhaps drilling was more like it. To make matters worse, when I called the school about Rachel kidnapping the kids, the assistant principal had informed me that Lindsay had probably missed half the semester, mainly because Rachel was too lazy to get her ass out of bed and take her each morning. She would never have that problem if it meant a mani/pedi or other pampering at the salon.

At some point, my letter went from fun to disappointing to eye opening. I began to play past events in my mind. I tried to picture

Rachel with the kids at home. Rachel with the kids at Mom and Dad's. Rachel and the kids out and about. Were there signs that I missed? Sure, I could offer up the excuse that I had been working out of town. But I couldn't with good conscience use that way of thinking to explain everything since we became parents. Was this my fault? Was I not around enough to be the dad the kids deserved? How could I not see something like this coming?

Beth must have sensed my frustration and dismay while finishing the letter, so she suggested we get out of the house. We would grab a bite to eat and do some clothes shopping for the kids, just in case.

On the way to the mall, I noticed Beth taking a different route. Then after a few more turns, I realized what we were doing. We pulled up in front of 8608 Penfield St, our childhood home. Beth knocked on the front door and explained to the current owners that we had lived there as kids and would love to take a look inside. Luckily, they were happy to oblige. Once inside, we sat down in the family room and made small talk with the owners. In my mind, I was picturing the times we all sat in front of the television and watched American Bandstand, The Ed Sullivan Show or college football on ABC with Keith Jackson. Not to mention laughing so hard with old reruns of Larry, Moe and Curly, the Three Stooges.

From there, Beth looked at her old room. Her old posters of David Cassidy and Don Drysdale were replaced by posters of Boyz II Men and Mike Piazza, hung by the girl now living in that room. I went into my old room, which was now their home office. I could almost hear Mom's voice yelling, "Mijos, dinner" and then Dad's piercing whistle followed by, "You heard your mother. Move, now!" Gil and I spent so many nights listening to Vin Scully and Chick Hearn after we were supposed to be sleeping. As I was heading back down the hallway, I passed by Mom and Dad's old room, and more recently, mine and Rachel's bedroom. I had such a hard time differentiating my childhood memories and memories with Rachel as an adult, both in this now strange looking house. I told Beth right then and there that we had to go. I didn't even bother to see if the pool looked the same. I was almost getting claustrophobic. What started out as a therapeutic pilgrimage turned into more than we bargained for. So we decided to head to dinner. Beth suggested Sizzler. I agreed without even realizing the possible ramifications of that idea.

When we walked in the door, just barely avoiding an early dinner rush, it was only then that I remembered that this is where I was planning on taking Rachel and the kids before I learned they were gone. I told Beth to order for me while I headed to the restroom. My face was as white as a ghost. I splashed some water on myself and got to our table. Grabbing a plate, I went to the salad bar to fill up on some badly needed roughage. Then I heard, "Daddy, can you help me, please?" And just as I was about to instinctively answer, the little girl's dad replied, "Sure, sweetie, what do you need?" I was sweating and shaking simultaneously. I needed more food and some water.

Back at our booth, Beth had already begun her meal. As I sat down, I noticed a dozen or so boys and girls, around eight years old, in what looked like their Little League uniforms. They were talking and laughing, racing up and down the restaurant aisles. I tried to bury my face in my steak and shrimp. Across the way, I saw a family of five, enjoying their meal. Two of the kids were harmlessly arguing like kids do, while the youngest was trying to negotiate with his parents for some more chocolate ice cream. It should have been a pretty picture. But it was pure anguish for me. Everywhere I looked, happy families. Children with smiling faces living their ordinary lives. Loud laughter, conversations resonating and getting louder. All of their voices, it felt like they were breathing on the back of my neck. To me, it looked like the rest of the world was carrying on in utopia while for me, life stopped at the most painful moment imaginable. I couldn't take it anymore and blurted out an agonizing, "No!"

Dishes and food flew off our table. The entire restaurant went silent, which made the echo of the glasses slamming on the floor even louder. My heart was shattering into a million pieces like the shards of glass on the tile floor. And as I went to gather my plates, I collapsed to the ground and began to sob like a little baby. I just didn't understand what I possibly did to deserve this. To the innermost part of my core, I truly believed I was a good person. I refused to believe that things this bad could happen to good people. I just couldn't understand. I became inconsolable. Beth took me in her arms and I wailed on her shoulder as she held my shaking body.

"Beth. Will I ever see them again? I just want to hold them one more time. Why Beth? Why did she do this to me? Why would someone want to put another person through this?"

"Rick, I wish like hell I had a good answer. But I'm here for you. The family is here for you. We will do everything in our power."

Beth's words became hard to understand as she also could no longer hold back her tears. And that made it tougher for our waitress to comprehend what we were going through, weeping in the middle of the now busy restaurant. Somehow, Beth explained to them the situation as best as she could. While there were dozens of concerned eyes staring at us, trying to figure out what was going on, they were nothing but faded background. I apologized profusely for the mess to the manager through hyperventilating breaths. I tried to pay the bill, and was surprised to find out the table next to us picked up the tab. This made me cry even harder, mainly out of gratitude for the display of humanity, but partly out of knowing that I had seemed so pathetic that people felt the need to pick up my tab. We picked up our things and hurried out of the restaurant and were soon walking through the hustle and bustle of the mall.

We staggered over to Macy's and began to browse the children's section, mostly sifting through outfits for Luke. Although, of course, I couldn't pass up a couple of dresses for the girls. Even though shopping was a good distraction, in my mind I was questioning everything. Why was God putting me through this? Why is life so hard? Are the kids healthy? Are they missing me? Naturally, I didn't have the answers and it left me absolutely empty inside. Then, like a lifesaving song, the cell phone rang.

"Rick, it's Bernie. Be at my office at 6 a.m. Let's go get them."

25
MISSION

Ever since I was a little kid, getting up early was always a chore for me. Mom always had to drag me out of bed to get ready for school. Fun stuff like soccer games and fishing trips, I still struggled to get going, even with my dad telling me to get my ass in gear. And of course, arriving before sunrise at the jobsite, let's just say I never showed up early. Getting up and ready that morning to pick up Bernie, I shot out of bed as if the spring in the mattress gave me a push. In fact, I was in the parking lot waiting on Bernie at 5:40 that morning before his Lexus showed up.

"Good morning, Daddy." Bernie said with a smile.

"I sure hope so, Bernie."

"You ready?"

"Bernie, you have no idea. I have never been more ready for anything in my life. Let's go."

The best thing about leaving so early was that we would touch down in Missouri just past 1 p.m. local time. But another indirect positive was that the 405 freeway was relatively empty at that time because it was just before rush hour, which allowed us to just beat the morning traffic. It was a quiet ride. I think I maybe said two words to Bernie the entire drive to the airport. Bernie tried to turn on the Mark and Brian radio show. I nixed that in favor of Howard Stern. Hearing him, Robin, Fred and the gang took my mind off the task at hand, at least for twenty minutes or so. Once at the ticket counter in LAX, I started to sweat. As I boarded the plane, I could feel my body begin to shake. We found our way to our seats. Despite the last minute fight, we were lucky enough to get the emergency exit row, and the middle seat between us was empty, so it gave us a little more room to stretch out. The flight was half empty. I guess not many people had a desire to go from the big city of Los Angeles to the small town middle of nowhere city of Joplin. As we departed, I dared to convince myself to try to get some sleep. After about ten minutes, I gave up on that notion. Bernie anticipated I would be restless, and that was an understatement for how I felt. So he handed me a couple of Field and Stream magazines. Perhaps a couple of bass fishing articles could pause my stressful mind. Instead, I found that the pages were turning louder than the pilot's announcements stating we were now at thirty thousand feet, with clear skies all the way to Joplin. Clear skies? Yeah right, I mumbled to myself. Famous last words. My leg started tapping the floor. Then my hand started tapping my leg. A few minutes later, Bernie's patience hit a road block and he handed me a drink.

"Here, drink this. Vodka. Neat."

I wanted Bernie to lay out a game plan. I was waiting for him to say something about what we were gonna do once we got there. I was hoping to rehearse it in my mind over and over so that I was ready to do what was needed. But Bernie just kept to himself for the most part. He was probably worried I would somehow blow this the way I almost did by talking to that evil bitch Elfrieda. Once in a while he would simply put a hand on my shoulder, assuring me that everything would be alright. The last thing I remember was feeling the burn in my throat from sipping a second Vodka neat. I don't know how it happened but I must have dozed off. Two hours later, the wheels touched down. We had landed.

The last time I was in Missouri, it was for Chad's funeral. As we left in the Chevy rental car, heading towards the hotel, I couldn't help but wonder what he would have thought about all this. Chad had this way of keeping Lindy in check. He said no, but in a way that didn't leave her feeling rejected. It was kind of a soft "no." Had Chad still been alive, who knows how these years here would have transpired. Would Lindy have gotten so mixed up in the church? Would she have reconnected with Dottie? Would Rachel have followed suit?

The lay of the land was exactly as I had remembered it some seven years before. Two-lane highways. Very few stop lights. There were only small, rundown motels, with the exception of the Holiday Inn we were checking into. And this was no ordinary Holiday Inn. Walking into the foyer, it was like the Taj Mahal. Crystal chandeliers were hanging from the high vaulted ceilings. The concierge and bell hops were dressed like they were serving for a five-hundred-dollar per plate event. There were marble counter tops at check-in. I had definitely never seen a Holiday Inn like this one, even in L.A. The stellar impression didn't stop there. The manager introduced himself to Bernie.

"Mr. Steinberg, welcome to the Joplin Holiday Inn. My name is Joe Turner. I take it your flight was nice."

"Yes Joe, thank you for checking on us. This is Rick. Let's make him feel welcome. Also, are there any messages?"

"Yes Mr. Steinberg. I have a message and a package for you right here. The rooms you requested are ready. Will you be needing any room service or anything else this evening?"

"No Joe. Not at the moment."

"Have a pleasant stay, gentlemen."

I was flabbergasted. Have a pleasant stay? All this non-nervousness made me nervous again as we made our way up to our adjoining rooms. Once inside, I asked what the message and the package were. First, Bernie read the message to himself. Then he used the phone in the room. It was a very vague conversation, but I deduced that he had to be talking with Scotty. After a few nonchalant exchanges, he hung up and opened the manila envelope. It contained what looked like some very thick documents. He scanned through them slowly, taking his sweet time as I waited with bated breath. I was like a dog anxiously awaiting the few crumbs that its owners drop from the dinner table. I couldn't take it anymore.

"Bernie! Say something!" I blurted out.

"Yes!" he exclaimed. "Rick, we got her."

"What do you mean? Rachel?"

"Yes Rachel. You will get your day in court tomorrow morning."

"You gotta be shitting me. How is that possible?"

"Hard to believe how quickly files must be carried out in Joplin to get an injunction. In Los Angeles, it usually takes a minimum of a week. But somehow, probably because this town is so damn small, the court order was filed within an hour, and shortly thereafter a notice to appear was delivered to Rachel. Tomorrow morning, 10:00 a.m. The kids will be there too."

"So, what do we do now Bernie?"

"We go have dinner and drinks and enjoy ourselves tonight. Things are falling into place. Now all we can do is hope for a judge that will give us a favorable ruling. But that is out of our control. I'm gonna go take a shower. Let's meet downstairs at 5 p.m."

Was this too good to be true? All of Bernie's instructions the past couple days, could it all really come to fruition? In my head, I thought, "No way!" I couldn't stop worrying that Rachel might go into hiding with the kids. Or would she show up and have the all-powerful judge in the palm of her hand like the instructor at our Subway training or the pastor at Lily of the Valley, or hell, like every other guy that walked on this planet? Would she really bring the kids? I couldn't shake the feeling that I may never see them again. That idea filled me with an overwhelming sense of dread. While I never truly blamed myself for what was going on, I would never forgive myself if Rachel did anything to harm them. The one memory that continued to haunt me was the time when Rachel insisted that Lindsay get the mail on a foul-weather afternoon in Oakhurst, despite the intimidating presence of a growling, slobbering Rottweiler awaiting outside that seemed deliriously hungry. How did I forget to put that memory in my letter to the court? I just couldn't find a way to shake my uneasiness and share in Bernie's nonchalant confidence. I went downstairs for a swim in the hotel's indoor pool to let off some steam before dinner. After a few laps, I stopped at the shallow end. I was at a crossroads. The pain, the torture, the struggle over the past few days, and all Bernie could tell me was that I'll get my day in court tomorrow. I wasn't buying it.

Nevertheless, I showered, put on some clothes and met Bernie at the hotel restaurant like we had planned. Another beautiful part of the hotel. This place was classy. It was like something out of a movie, a real swanky joint, with dim lighting, a grand piano, and the sweet and delicious smell of fresh baked bread coming out of the oven. We got our table and Bernie was quick to order a scotch, while I settled with my typical beer. To my liking, it was ice cold. Then, dinner. Perhaps the best chicken fried steak I had ever had with a big side of buttery mashed potatoes. Bernie made a mess of his half rack of ribs, St. Louis style. Comfort food. What else would you expect in that part of the country? There were only a few guests in the restaurant by the time the piano player started to play. But to my surprise, it was Bernie who started performing, if you can call it that.

"Bartender, three fingers of the best scotch you have for my good friend, the piano player. What is your name sir?" I heard Bernie begin.

"Just call me Slick. Thank you, kind sir. What are you gentlemen celebrating?"

"We are celebrating life. And family. Say, do you take requests?" Bernie asked as he slipped a five-dollar bill across the top of the Baby Grand.

Slick raised his drink toward Bernie and explained, "Sir, you name it. I'll play it. What's your pleasure?"

"How about, 'Let's call the whole thing off' the Louis Armstrong version."

"Good choice Mr.?"

"Steinberg. Bernie Steinberg."

Then Bernie sat back down with his scotch and began bouncing back and forth with the rhythm of the tune. After a while, he just couldn't hold back any longer. He got right up there next to Slick and started singing with him. I kind of shook my head, but couldn't help but smirk. This was the guy I was putting all my trust in. The guy who I was hoping would get my kids back. This was my voice of reason, and here he is bellowing along, completely ruining a classic. Then as he sang, "You say to-may-toe. I say to-mah-toe," he gave me a big grin and yelled out at me, "Relax, Rick. Have another beer!" And so I did.

At that moment I finally realized what my genius of a lawyer was doing. Not only was he helping me to have a good time, which was something I hadn't had in weeks (or maybe months thanks to Rachel), but he was also trying to put me and my worried mind at ease. And it was beginning to work. A couple songs later and it was my turn to make a request.

"Slick, you know country music?"

"Kind sir, need I remind you where you are? You are sitting in the Bible Belt at its finest. Ain't no piano player worth a lick who can't sing country music. What can I play for you?"

"Because your playing is so sweet, and because I long for the beach I grew up with, can you please play Marina Del Rey by George Strait?"

"Coming right up. Cheers to you."

As the notes started playing, it was perfection to my ears. At that moment I was convinced. No one and nothing was going to keep me from my kids. Not the judge, not religion, and certainly not my spoiled bitch wife and her brainwashing birthmother.

26
RESCUE

Despite a full night's rest, I was extremely agitated and nervous when Bernie rang my hotel room. He noticed the troubled grimace on my face and offered a consoling, "Stay calm." As usual, a statement like that didn't help much. I was able to keep down a biscuit from the complimentary continental breakfast on our way out the door to our appointed court date. As we approached the car, it looked like a storm was brewing, like rain was going to dump on us at any moment.

All the while, I was hoping Rachel spent the night tossing and turning wondering what she might be in for. I couldn't remember if Rachel ever had to fight for anything in her undisciplined life. I couldn't imagine what that would even look like. Then of course my mind drifted to the kids again. How would they look? Scotty had filled us in on Rachel's life the past few days and how she was ignoring the kids' normal needs. As much as I was dying to see them and hold them again, I was bracing myself for the worst.

Inside the courthouse's decent-sized hall, I tried desperately to stand up straight. But every bone in my body trembled and my knees struggled not to buckle beneath me. Bernie led me to a nearby bench and reminded me once again to calm down. It was difficult to calm down, especially when the judge entered the court room. He was a tall man of what looked to be six-foot-three, gray hair only around his temple, with an extremely commanding presence. I gingerly sat down, but was brought to my feet when I heard the familiar sound of gibberish words that only a baby boy of eighteen months would blurt out.

With tears in my eyes I exclaimed, "That's my son! That's Luke."

"How do you know?" The judge responded.

"Because that's my son. I know my son. If you have someone go out and look, there should be three kids with either their mom and aunt or their mom and grandmother."

And something in the judge's smile told me that he was a decent and fair man of the court. In fact, he casually pretended to go outside for a cup of coffee. Thirty seconds later, he reappeared. "Ok, you're right. They're coming in now and then we'll begin."

Another minute went by, and for a moment, I couldn't bring myself to look back to the doorway. But then I heard a loud echo as the giant court doors swung open. And then another wonderful sound. "Daddy! Daddy!"

It was Lindsay! Before they even got all the way into the court room, she spotted me. Her yelp grabbed Aubrey's attention, whose eyes lit up. The two sprung free from their Aunt Lindy's grip and darted down the passageway straight to me. At the same time that Rachel and Lindy's jaws dropped to floor, my heart melted at the sight of my two precious little girls. I held out my arms as they fearlessly leapt into my warm embrace. I was so ecstatic at being able to hold my children again that I never even noticed the evil glare Rachel was giving me. I no longer cared about her or whether I ever would see her again. All that mattered was that I was hugging my kids once again! I would never let them go.

I'm not sure if it was on purpose, but Rachel and Lindy made it impossible to see Luke from where I was standing with the girls. They were still standing at the entrance to the courtroom, which was about 100 feet away from Bernie and I. Rachel's attorney, an attractive brunette with a short, neatly-styled bob, confidently approached Bernie and introduced herself. "Counselor, I'm Rhonda Matthews, representing Ms. Martinez. Shall we recuse ourselves to a private room?"

Bernie nodded to me, signifying that it was typical protocol to hammer out some kind of deal before entering the judge's chambers. I refused to let go of Lindsay and Aubrey, who were begging to go home with me. I was only convinced to join the discussion when Rhonda agreed that the girls could come with us into the room.

When Rachel entered, I of course was expecting the worst. Her demeanor was not typical Rachel. She normally stood tall and exuded confidence. But this time she seemed almost sheepish. And then she absolutely shocked me by offering up the best deal I could have ever dreamed of. Following a few terse pleasantries, Rhonda disclosed that Rachel was willing to relinquish the kids, but under several circumstances:

"First, Rick would have to absolve Rachel of all debt the two had acquired as a couple."

Then Rachel, matter of fact and righteously interrupted, slamming her finger down on the table with each demand as if she were in a position of power, "This means all the back taxes from selling our house, and all of the maxed out credit cards. And also, the children must always have premium, top-of-the-line medical insurance."

She went on and on with absurd demands, insisting I must also mail her the clothes that she left in the closet, as well as her jewelry. Her sense of entitlement was outrageous, as if she was the one who traveled thousands of miles to get what she wanted. I waited. And waited some more. Finally, after what felt like an eternity, her laundry list of demands ended. Without a thought, I agreed to it all. I was so thankful for the offer that I even agreed to send pictures of the kids on a regular basis. Mostly, just to appease her and to kiss her now-widening ass for what I hoped was one final time.

I felt like the king of the world. I got everything I wanted. I could take the kids home, and because Rachel granted me full custody, I never had to see her again. I could not be happier. As I opened the courthouse doors and was headed to meet Lindy to get Luke, I was surprised to see that the rain clouds had dissipated and the sky was perfectly cloudless and blue, sun shining down on my cheeks as if God were smiling upon me. Nothing could put a damper on this day.

But my overwhelming elation took a wicked turn when Bernie and I approached Lindy's car to take possession of the items my soon-to-be-ex had so thoughtlessly ran off with with a few days earlier. At first, I couldn't help but chuckle to myself as I approached Lindy's faded-orange Chevy Vega. This was the same old jalopy that Lindy drove in Los Angeles back when Rachel and I began dating some fourteen years earlier. A slightly gray-hair Lindy was standing next to her car, holding Luke in her arms. Rachel, who had given such a defiant demonstration just ten minutes prior, was now cowering alone inside the government building, behind the entrance with the revolving door. Her attorney's presence no longer provided the added support that made her feel so empowered. Shocking, and yet not shocking at the same time, Rachel had childishly sent Lindy out to handle the offspring transfer. Just as she had so easily left Luke while he was in the hospital with pneumonia, she was again all too happy to pass her motherly responsibilities off to someone else.

As we approached the car, the rusting coupe's rear hatch was propped open, revealing to me the unbelievable sight of three suitcases, already packed for shipment. 'Rachel had used the kids as bargaining chips,' I thought, 'she had every intention of handing them over once her price was met.' It didn't matter whether or not I had even come to Missouri; Just like her mother had done to her, Rachel was ready to give away the kids. She probably would have handed them off to strangers…for the right amount of money.

Lindsay and Aubrey, who had been escorted out of chambers before final negotiations began, rose up from the back seat of the car as soon as they heard me removing their luggage. I was surprised they could pop up so easily from their car seats. It was only then that I realized there weren't any. I shouldn't have been surprised by this, but I found myself staring at Lindy in disgust. "Really, Lindy? I'm supposed to transport my kids to the airport without child seats?"

"There's one in front for Luke," she snorted. "We've had to go without car seats for the girls, so you'll just have to do the same." I could only shake my head. They couldn't have bought a couple of car seats with my $23000? The Parker women were selfish and careless through and through.

Luke had been squirming to get out of Lindy's embrace from the moment he spotted me, and after I finished packing my son's belongings into our newer, safer rental car, Luke's arms were outstretched, desperately awaiting my love, which he had clearly missed so much.

"Wow," I uttered as I took Luke from Lindy. I had placed my hands on the baby's bulging diaper. "That's one heavy load you're carrying, buddy." Although I had wrongly assumed that Rachel would provide me with all the necessary car seats, thankfully I did prepare a baby bag for Luke with the anticipation of our long journey home. After placing Luke on the front seat of the car, I grabbed a new diaper from the bag, pulled off the soiled garment and gasped in utter repulsion. Luke's genital region was bright red, extremely raw and severely chafed. The lack of proper care and hygiene astonished me.

"Damn it!" I fumed. "You and Rachel, Dottie, the Brother and your God are severely twisted if this is what you think is the right way to take care of a baby. My God would never treat children this way."

Lindy shut the hatchback door and walked away without uttering a word. There was nothing she could say. I was right, and for the first time since I saw her that morning, her face showed just a little bit of regret. And while she had done a piss-poor job of protecting her nieces and nephew, the majority of the blame belonged to Rachel. Kids aren't supposed to be there for their mother. A mother is supposed to be there for her kids. And Rachel wasn't. She hadn't been for a long time. And she should be the one to take my lecture and venting. Instead, as we were pulling out of the courthouse parking lot, I saw in the rearview mirror a beaming Rachel, nearly skipping out of the courthouse doors, clearly relieved and thrilled to be free.

Bernie pulled out a legal pad and was about to start jotting things down, just in case Rachel changed her mind about the child custody agreement. Our drive to the airport was about to be filled with horror stories, recounted by Lindsay and Aubrey, about their Joplin experiences with Rachel. However, I just wanted to focus on being a family once again. But then:

"Daddy, Daddy!" Lindsay bellowed. "Mommy said if we didn't believe in God, that our ears and hands would fall off." Then Aubrey's tiny voice added, "Yeah, Mommy was mean."

Bernie looked over at me and whispered, "We got to these kids just in time." I responded clear as day, "Let's get the hell out of this town and go home."

27
HOME

My watch read 3:07 in the afternoon when the plane took off, officially leaving Joplin and jetting back to California. Much like the settlers did generations ago, we were heading west, looking for greener pastures. Well, in this case, we were getting out of dodge. Bernie, the kids, and I were returning to the normalcy of Los Angeles, ridding ourselves of the bizarre happenings in Anytown, USA. The plane was half empty on the flight to Missouri. This Boeing 747 was half full. I had the whole row to myself with the kids. Bernie was across the aisle. The hours flew by, mostly because we all just played and talked the whole time. We took turns passing Luke around like a hot potato, going from my lap, then sitting between the girls.

The loud, screeching of the wheels sounded like a symphony as the plane hit the tarmac. And as we exited the cabin, I let out a big sigh, and a couple of tears fell from my eyes. We couldn't wait to get home, but before we exited the terminal, there was one call I had to make. I found the nearest public pay phone because in the rush to get to Missouri, I had forgotten my cell phone at home. I could feel my body trembling as I put those coins in that pay phone and dialed that number.

"Mom…we got the kids." I could hear her voice cracking with tears of joy.

"Honey! Rick got the kids!" They let out a big and triumphant yell. "Where are you now, mijo? How are the kids?"

"We're about to leave LAX and head home. If you guys could drive down…" Dad got on the phone and interrupted me.

"We'll all be over midday tomorrow. The entire famiy. We can't wait to see our grandchildren again."

The smog of the Southland had never smelled so wonderful to me. I offered Bernie a ride back to his Encino office but he insisted on taking a cab. He let me know that I should just be with the kids. Both Lindsay and Aubrey ran over to him and said, "Bye Uncle Bernie. Thank you!" and gave him a big hug. A few tears rolled down his normally composed face. Then, Bernie did something I never thought he would do. He gave me a hug. And just before he entered the cab, he turned to me and commented, "I have never seen a father interact with their kids as wonderfully as you do. You are truly a great parent. I am so happy for you that you got them back. You deserve all the happiness in the world. Shame on her, Rick." And just like that, he was gone.

After getting the luggage, as we approached our car, I asked the kids what they wanted for dinner. Both Lindsay and Aubrey shouted, "McDonald's, Daddy. Can we have McDonald's?"

"Kids, tonight, you can have anything you want."

Once we arrived back home, Lindsay absolutely floored me when she said, "Daddy, the place is so clean."

"Yep, tomorrow you can thank your Auntie Beth."

That first night, we all ate at the dinner table, as a family once again. Then, one by one, I bathed the kids and threw their badly stained clothes in the trash. After the baths, I put them all in their new Macy's pajamas, and we all gathered in the living room to watch "The Little Mermaid." I sat on the couch and just watched them. Watched them watch TV. Watched Luke get into everything. Watched Lindsay and Aubrey giggle at the cartoon and sing along with Ariel. This would be the first of many mental photos I took that are forever ingrained in my mind. After the movie, I actually moved Luke's crib into my room and rolled out the girls' sleeping bags at the foot of my bed.

It was just before 9, and I wanted to check to see how the kids were feeling. "Kids, is there anything you want to say? Anything you want to ask me about what happened and what's next?" No answer from any of the kids. I continued, "You see kids, Daddy loves you so much and I was so sad when I couldn't..." And all I could hear was snoring. All three of them were out like a light. The mental and emotional exhaustion finally caught up with them. In that quiet moment, with my children near me peacefully sleeping, I looked up and said, "Thank you, God." And with that, I drifted off to sleep.

I woke up at half past four on that Sunday morning. With the kids still sound asleep, I put on a pot of coffee. There was one more looming task I had to take care of. I went downstairs and gathered the boxes of bills, as well as the documents Bernie gave me from the court proceedings. I also grabbed that same calculator I used when counting the seconds until Dad had arrived the week prior. A few hours of adding and sifting through everything, I had what I wanted. The total of all the bills Rachel left me with, added with the back taxes I now assumed, plus figuring in the penalties and late fees from not being able to pay it all back at once. Bottom line, Lindsay, Aubrey and Luke were sold by their mother to me for just over $215,000.

Surprisingly, the kids didn't wake up until almost eleven, and just as I was about to start breakfast, there was a knock at the door. The entire family was there. Mom and Dad. Beth, Gil and their families. It was an ambush of epic proportions. Beth had all the food for a barbecue like we used to have at the Penfield house. Mom and Dad had dozens of presents for the kids, but nowhere near the amount of hugs and kisses they gave them that day. As I looked at the pure joy on my children's faces, something deep inside warned me that there would be repercussions down the line of what Rachel had done with and to the kids. Especially to Lindsay and Aubrey. Who knows just how much of that godforsaken place they would remember? But for today, I wasn't going to worry about that.

A few minutes went by before Gil pulled me aside. "Just wanted to check on you Rick. How are you feeling?" I let out a deep breath, "Someday, I'll tell you all about it." He understood and gave me a great, big bear hug. "Come on chump. Let's eat."

I was floored by the family's outpouring of love. I hugged everyone individually, thanking them for all of their support. Luke was particularly popular, cooing and laughing as he was passed from person to person. I was totally caught off guard when Dad hollered from out on the patio for everyone's attention. I could feel the tears welling up in my eyes as I focused on the man I had tried so desperately to impress all throughout my life. Dad took a step toward me. Just as I reached out to hug him, he held up his hand to stop me. "Son, I just want to say I am so very proud of you." By now, I was arm and arm with both Mom and Beth. There was a distinct "Aw" heard from the group as he continued. "Your mom and I have always loved you, but the effort you showed in bringing these kids back home, we have never been prouder. You truly are a great man. To Rick and the kids." Tears were flowing from everyone, in between the loud cheers and the jubilant laughter. I turned to Beth and Mom, and told them both how much I loved them and how much I appreciated all they did. And before I walked away, I turned back and said, "Hey, I almost forgot. Happy Mother's Day."

Printed in the United States
By Bookmasters